The laidback lifestyle and moderate climate of the Doon Valley and its surrounding environs make it the ideal retirement destination that it is. Some parts of the town in this region still retain a distinctive British character, while several have outgrown their colonial origins, transforming the area from an unhurried summer retreat to the bustling capital of a newly formed state.

This anthology captures the unique flavour of the region—both its old-world charm and the newer characteristics that now define parts of it. Most of the contributors to this volume have lived in the valley long enough to witness the changes that have taken place. There is nostalgia here, and history too, and the social change. All the writers have lived in Doon and love the city and write about a region that has shaped them.

*Once Upon a Time in the Doon ...* includes writings by eminent authors, and also by gifted people, who write entertainingly but whose occupations prevent them from becoming full-time writers. They may have spent the greater part of their lives in the district, or they may have discovered it comparatively recently. Either way, their own personality traits have a bearing on the subject, and the result is a variety of views and viewpoints. The richness and diversity of the Doon is captured in these personal stories and vignettes.

This book is of interest to one who has journeyed through the valley and explored it. It will be doubly so to those who have lived in it.

**Ruskin Bond**, well-known as one of India's best-loved and most prolific writers, has been writing novels, poetry, essays and short stories for almost half a century now. Apart from this, over the years he has expertly compiled and edited a number of anthologies. For his outstanding literary contribution, Ruskin Bond has been conferred the John Llewellyn Rhys Memorial Prize in 1957, the Sahitya Akademi award in 1992 (for English writing in India), and the Padma Shri by the Government of India in 1999.

# Once Upon a Time in the Doon...

*Writings from the Green Valley*

*Edited by*

Ruskin Bond

RUPA

Published by
Rupa Publications India Pvt. Ltd 2007
161-B/4, Gulmohar House,
Yusuf Sarai Community Centre,
New Delhi 110049

*Sales centres:*
Bengaluru Chennai
Hyderabad Kolkata Mumbai



P-ISBN: 978-81-291-1620-8

E-ISBN: 978-81-291-2668-9

Sixth impression 2026

10 9 8 7 6



Printed in India

*This book is dedicated to the memory of*
*David Keeling*

*We are indeed, fortunate to receive his last piece,*
*and salute his enthusiasm for this anthology*

# Contents

# Introduction

The Doon Valley and the adjoining hills are bordered by the Ganga to the east and the Jamuna to the west, a situation that ought to afford the district a certain sanctity. But the Doon is known as a centre of learning and instruction. The Forest Research Institute, the Indian Military Academy, the Survey of India, and the many famous schools in Dehra Dun and Mussoorie, give the Doon its unique character.

This presents an interesting conundrum. Does one have to be situated on the banks of a river, or in sight of it, to absorb some of its sanctity? The temples and sacred places are all up-river—Badrinath, where the Alaknanda rises; Gangotri, where the Bhagirathi is born, Kedarnath between them; and Jumnotri at the source of the Jamuna. And downstream on the Ganga, Rishikesh and Haridwar absorb a multitude of pilgrims.

From where I stand, on a spur of the Landour–Mussoorie range, I find that all springs, streams and rivulets flow to the left and become tributaries of the Ganga, while all those to the right eventually find their way to the Jamuna. This then is the perfect watershed. But, of course, geography and religion do not necessarily coincide. On this spur are a number of schools—temples of learning, one might call them—several of them established over a hundred years ago, and more in demand with the young India of today than they were in the past.

The valley and the mountain provide several sharp contrasts; climate and geography come into the picture again. The Doon is sub-tropical, the flora completely at variance with the temperate growth of the Himalayan foothills. So, while the Mussoorie range is clothed with oak, deodar, pine, rhododendron and horse-chestnut, Dehra Dun has its jacaranda and laburnum, its forests of sal and shisham, and its mango, *litchi* and papaya orchards.

Or, at least it did. The orchards, sadly have given way to housing estates, and the day may not be far off when there will be no *litchis* growing in the Doon. Like the famed Basmati rice of Dehra, it will have to be brought in from elsewhere.

We still have the Rajaji Sanctuary, with its rich variety of trees, but even here the forest cover seems to have thinned out over the years. And alas, there are no longer any tigers in these jungles. They were all shot in the days just before and after Independence, when poaching was at its peak and jeeps could take the forest tracks and penetrate deep into the jungle.

There were tigers aplenty in the days of my youth. My Uncle Ken, who was terrified of big cats, was persuaded to accompany a party of *shikaris* into the forests near Haridwar. But he declined to join them on this hunt for a tiger. Instead, he remained behind in the forest rest house, taking care to close all the doors and windows. This done, he retired to a bedroom, only to find a handsome, full-grown leopard asleep at the foot of one of the beds. Uncle Ken shot out of the nearest window and ran for the safety of the forest.

Although I did my schooling Shimla, my holidays were spent in Dehra Dun, and most of my friends went to St Joseph's

Academy, a school which has served the residents of the town, for seventy-five years. Our favourite haunts were the *Chaatwala Gali,* the Sulphur Springs (then a wilderness), the Robber's Cave, the Odeon Cinema (now gone), and the old bridle-path to Mussoorie; this last we covered on foot whenever we wanted to visit the hill station.

Recently, I wrote a poem about the old footpath, and as one or two readers had enjoyed it, I reproduce it here to add to the introduction and give you a flavour of a Doon boyhood...

### *Remember the Old Road*

*Remember the old road,*
*The steep stony path*
*That took us up from Rajpur,*
*Toiling and sweating*
*And grumbling at the climb,*
*But enjoying it all the same.*
*At first the hills were hot and bare,*
*But then there were trees near Jharipani*
*And we stopped at the Halfway House*
*And swallowed lungfuls of diamond-cut air.*
*Then onwards, upwards, to the town,*
*Our appetites to repair!*

*Well, no one uses the old road any more.*
*Walking is out of fashion now.*
*And if you have a car to take you*
*Swiftly up the motor-road*
*Why bother to toil up a disused path?*
*You'd have to be an old romantic like me*

*To want to take that route again.*
*But I did it last year,*
*Pausing and plodding and gasping for air—*
*Both road and I being a little worse for wear!*
*But I made it to the top and stopped to rest*
*And looked down to the valley and the silver stream*
*Winding its way towards the plains.*
*And the land stretched out before me, and the years fell away,*
*And I was a boy again,*
*And the friends of my youth were there beside me,*
*And nothing had changed.*

Over the years, Dehra Dun has grown from a small garden town into a bustling mini-city, the capital of Uttarakhand. Unlike Delhi and some other cities, its growth is circumscribed by its geographical situation, for which we must be grateful to the two great rivers, Ganga and Jamuna. Thus far, they say, and no further!

Most of the contributors to this volume have lived in the Doon long enough to witness the changes that have taken place. There is nostalgia here, and history too, and social change.

The collection includes writings by some well-known authors, and also by gifted people who write entertainingly but whose occupations prevent them from becoming full-time writers. They may have spent the greater part of their lives in the district, or they may have discovered it comparatively recently. Either way, they bring their own personalities to bear on the subject, and the result is a variety of views and viewpoints. The richness and diversity of the Doon is captured in these personal stories and vignettes.

During the preparation of this anthology I met Deepali Jain, who was kind and enthusiastic enough to help out with the compilation.

Shortly after submitting his entertaining contribution to this anthology, David Keeling reached the end of his 'long and winding road'. He passed away in a Delhi hospital, much to the dismay of his many friends in Dehra Dun and Mussoorie.

David was a friendly, convivial gentleman, always curious about his surroundings, and eager to be friends with anyone who had done something interesting. He was a frequent visitor to Sister's Bazaar, Landour, after stopping at my place on his way up, to talk about books, cricket, and local history.

Rajpur, where he lived, won't be the same without him.

Ruskin Bond
August, 2007

# That Long and Winding Road

David Keeling

The Rajpur Road, that long and winding road journeys from the clock tower to Rajpur village. Then, and now, it forms the very backbone of this emerging city. Having seen Dehra in all its former glory, the base of this spine travels Northwest with many ribs housing new estates; through squalor and splendour to culminate in Rajpur village before joining the old road to Mussoorie. Tree-lined—it was with grand old houses and wide boulevards. No longer! The sprawl of urban development has made it unrecognisable from its former self. Encroachments and the interminable and apparently uncontrollable traffic, the latter with tempos, trucks, buses and cars vying with two-wheelers for space. But still, squeezed between the high rise and the shopping malls remain some lovely old compounds. Emerging after the Mussoorie bypass the road continues steeply upwards through pleasanter surroundings with remaining trees and stately if not altogether elegant houses. There is no apparent planning permission required for whatever monstrosity one wishes to construct. At the top of the road, the apex, there is Rajpur village. But more of that later. To the present—

*I think that I shall never see*
*a billboard lovely as a tree.*
*Perhaps, unless the billboards fall*
*I'll never see a tree at all.*

Ogden Nash 'Song of the open road' 1933.

In 1933, the sight of a billboard or hoarding on this long and winding boulevard or in the hills of Mussoorie would have been unthinkable. Not to say ludicrous. Then the Rajpur Road was guarded on both sides by trees giving shade and comfort to the pedestrian. There was little vehicular traffic. It takes a great deal of imagination to conjure up how Dehra must have changed from that small sleepy and quaint town into the present-day architectural disaster. A great deal of profiteering by the unscrupulous land-grabbers to cater to the out-of-towners was needed to achieve this. But achieve it they have and created the unthinkable, the unspeakable. The ultimate urban slum!

Doon's Rajpur Road begins at the inevitable clock tower, built as so many were, in the 1930s. All townships in the hill-side region have one. As do most other townships in North India. Villages would begin with a few shops, followed by a police *chowki*, the court, a lock-up, places of worship and then the clock-tower. Whether, to denote its importance, or to provide a directional bearing or simply and more likely, to enable good citizens to tell the time (few people had watches then) is a matter for conjecture. But no township would be complete without its

clock-tower. Not all have survived, particularly the one in Tehri which was slowly and relentlessly submerged along with the old city by the river Bhagirathi to form the Tehri Dam. The clock-tower was the last to go. Its roof sticking incongruously from the insidiously encroaching waters. The clock did not suffer the same ignominy. Some entrepreneurial characters purloined or nicked it before the waters could take their toll. But depart it did without a farewell ding or dong. Probably, in the back of a tempo. Waste not, want not.

Proceeding north up this long and winding road, the old-style colonial offices and houses have been torn down and replaced by a higgledy-piggledy collection of small shops, offices and doctor's surgeries in rather primitive conditions. In contrast to the modern centre for the state postal services with its garish fountain, the Post Master General's house higher up on the road is unchanged. Built in brick and wood with extensive gardens. It is haunted!

A quiet supper with Mrs Suneeta Trivedi, then Chief Post Master General for tales from the past, both mine and hers. The compound spreads over five acres. The estate garden once had *litchi* and mango trees now depleted by a declining underground water table. Then, leopards and panthers roamed unchecked. Now, only monkeys. It has a history. Built in approximately 1887–88 by the then Maharaja of Sohara, a place near Bijnor, UP, it was constructed in keeping with the tradition of Hindu royalty of maintaining two households. One, where principles, vegetarian food and purdah were strictly observed. The other, for entertainment and social compatibility with the Raj. In legend the house was built, by the Maharaja for his eighteen year-old mistress, Roshanara. Said to be half-Dutch with a Jewish background, her beauty had become the toast of Dehra Dun cantonment, desired by Englishmen and Indian royalty alike.

After the Maharaja, the mistress stayed on until she died mysteriously and was apparently buried on the estate. Still, we are told, to rise, roam and moan through the roses dressed in a white skirt with big floral patterns. A *maali*, who lived to be ninety-six years, swears to seeing the real *'Gori memsaab'* in her haunting habit. The legend continues. I scurried away before midnight. Lest the ghost of Roshanara fancied me.

It is easy to see how far the desecration of Doon has reached. Past the Osho fast food restaurant made popular by local school boys, the shopping malls nearing stages of completion, the trees that were hacked down to make way for modernity replaced by some token bougainvillea. The avenue of old trees begins again. The Survey of India housed in the lovely Hathibarkala estate. Opposite is the National Institute for the Visually Handicapped and the Central Braille Press. Next, approaches the President's Bodyguard. Here, there are no obvious encroachments on the vast tracts of virgin land. Woe betide any developer who tries it on with these august organisations.

When I was posted in Seychelles, I was fascinated by an obviously five star hotel on the beach which had neither sun-bathers nor people in the restaurant. I asked the Manager over a drink why his hotel was doing badly and was somewhat astonished when he said they were always full. 'This is,' he said 'a place for the newly weds and the nearly deads.' Neither category got out of bed even for room-service and in the evening they would sit on their balconies looking at the sea, coddling and canoodling, not too far removed from their favourite piece of furniture. The bed. Dehra Dun used to be like that when street lights became superfluous after seven in the evening. But has it changed? Not much. My lady personal bank manager, Anshu tells me that few young people go out in the evenings except to each other's houses. On Sundays, they might drive or picnic; in summer, a swim in the stream at Robber's Cave or Lacchiwala. But both lack privacy and one is more than likely to find giggling village children peering through the bushes hoping for a glimpse of naked flesh. In Dehra city the young men mainly use the evenings to play billiards or snooker in one of the many seedy joints which abound in some of the dingier streets, or carrom in one of the coffee or *chai* houses. The cosmopolitan Doon young has seen the arrival of the coffee shop. Barista is one such meeting place of a few groups of young people and quite often, couples. Innovatively attached to a book shop. So, one can buy a book and read it over the many variations of the cup of coffee. Some, bereft of a loved one, string a guitar to themselves and wish. Even these coffee shops are losing their novelty and are now more often seen empty. The ties, if not the attractions of home and family seem to win out over the semi-illicit assignations in a dark corner over a cappuccino. A few hopefuls have opened so-called trendy bistro's. These fare even less well. The Mughlai Kitchens, K.C. Soup Bar, Café Day offer culinary hopes which are rarely fulfilled. The food is generally a limited variation of the real thing served in their Delhi or Mumbai counterparts. The shopping malls are for browsing, not buying, their attraction being air-conditioning in the summer and warmth in winter.

Past the village at Jakhan at the Mussoorie bypass is the centre for dance and music, 'Ghungroo' run by noted Kathak exponent Mrs Promila Pande. A few shops dealing in 'antiques' mark the diversion towards Malsi on the new Mussoorie Road. As one continues on the Rajpur Road, one enters the land of the once powerful but mainly retired civil servants and military officials. They are inveterate walkers, both in the mornings and late afternoons, which is why the road was christened 'the road of green trees and white hair'. Here, the plots of land remain largely undivided although further down the hill towards the now empty water bed of the Rispana an enterprising few sighting a fast buck have built less than desirable residences which cling to the hillside cheek by jowl. It is on this stretch of road that one can see at night, the necklace of sparkling Mussoorie lights, separated safely by a vast swathe of reserved forest mountains. Living on the other side of the Rajpur spur to the south and west, one may be lucky to gain a panoramic view of the Shivaliks. This is temple land. The Ramakrishna Mission and the very popular Sai Baba temple. A meeting place for devotees, principally on Thursdays and Sundays. As in most religious organisations or foundations, the Sai Baba temple is a weekly event, an outing for families who doff their shoes and donn their finest garments before offering prayers and swapping homespun gossipy stories with their neighbours. But even the Sai Baba temple, especially in the early mornings and late afternoons is sadly bereft of devotees. Despite artificial illumination, it seems quietly to sleep in the heat of the summer while providing an ideal film setting for the haunted house during the lashings offered by the Gods during the monsoon.

Nearby is the Sakya temple. One of the four schools of Tibetan Buddhism, widely popular and populous. His Holiness Sakya presides and is quite amenable to visitors. The Sakya Buddhists are unusual in that although paying respect to the Dalai Lama their tradition of succession is hereditary. Many devotees inhabit the Rajpur village, a sizeable township. They live in harmony with their Hindu neighbours although there is less social inter-activity. There are recorded cases of inter-marriage by Tibetan Buddhists outside their community, but not in the closed non-secular society in Dehra Dun. His Holiness said, proudly, that he has two sons. A sister living in Canada has four, the oldest of whom married a Japanese girl and the third's father-in-law is Scottish with a Philippine wife. Perhaps, outside their family-oriented lifestyle in India, the Tibetans feel freer to chance their arm.

Rajpur village is on the top of a steep hill, where the Rajpur Road peters out. There is a First World War memorial which records that seventy-nine men went to the 'Great War' and xxx returned. One must assume that they all got the chop somewhere on the battlefields of France. Lastly, one reaches the police *chowki*, one of the earliest established by the British and which still maintains its original building, constructed with the establishment of a force in 1850. Here, the police confirm the lack, or is it apathy, of communal violence between the two communities. Disputes comprise in the main marriage and land or both. A case of a wife-to-be who failed to turn up for her *shaadi*. She had eloped with someone who had more landholding than the disconsolate jilted groom. Land disputes would fill another book for Job and certainly marriage is covered by the Ten Commandments. The latter mentions not the Eleventh Commandment 'Thou shalt not get found out'.

In Rajpur, live Lt Gen (Retd) Shamsher Singh and his wife Honey and their daughter Cherie. Shamsher has some good stories about when he was Indian Defence advisor in Moscow. Although his command of Russian is about the same as mine over Hindi. Confined to the basics of life: booze, food, 'bed, book and candle'. Although the candle is more necessary in our power- poor state of Uttarakhand. Next door to the Shamsher Singh's is an old people's home where some seventy or eighty couples and singles live in retirement. Each have their own miniscule flat but with good security and an office manager. Their constraint is mobility. The road to Rajpur village has a steepish gradient for old people and there are no helpful traders who would come, even occasionally, to sell fruit, vegetables and household necessities. But they seem a happy and hospitable crowd. People in their later years rarely groan and moan as much as the young.

Halfway between the Rajpur bypass turnoff and the Rajpur village is my humble establishment. Set in a little over two *bighas,* it is essentially an English style country cottage with plenty of windows and *jaali* doors which open to allow the breeze. They also admit a host of *keedas* of varying sizes and species. These are hungrily gobbled up by two tame geckos, to whom I remain eternally grateful. I have not yet seen a snake in the garden, although cobras and rat-snakes do abound. This, I attribute to the advice of the swami who blessed the cottage on its completion. He insisted that two silver cobras be planted, or rather entombed in the foundations. My accountant added my business card encased in cellophane, lest there should be any dispute over ownership. So far, both the cobras have, touchwood, accomplished their task very well. But I cannot for the life of me remember in which part of the foundations they are encased. Thanks to the alluvial soil, washed down from the Himalayas, the garden is a haven for flowers, fruit trees and vegetables of all kinds. There are, of course, monkeys of which I have a dislike mixed with fear. Freddie, my Labrador's, favourite pass-time apart from sleeping is chasing these animals. Although, he would be as surprised as I, if ever he caught one.

The long and winding road now lives up to its name in the tortuitous ascent up to Mussoorie. Much more comprehensively chronicled by the aficionado Ruskin Bond. Once, Rajpur was the staging post for intrepid travellers prepared to walk through the jungles and forests to the 6,000 ft Mussoorie hill station. For the less hardy, there were 'palankeens' normally carried by six *coolies*. For the weak-legged or faint-hearted, mules and horses. The introduction of a new road and subsequently a bypass and the motor car led Mussoorie to be a more accessible hill station and a summer abode for the rich and famous. The road was once precarious, but is now safely guarded by retaining walls from all but the most outrageous and often inebriated drivers from the plains who, perhaps thinking they are in Europe, tend to drive on the right, especially around hairpin bends. Some of the Mussoorie grand houses remain. The Skinner sisters at Sikander Hall in Barlowganj maintain their modest but high standards and a wide circle of friends. Even higher in Landour and in Sisters bazaar, established owners have resisted the lure of lucre and preserved their historic traditions. But Mussoorie has basically been turned, like Shimla, into an urban dump. Much has been written about the few remaining characters who still live there. The Rajmata of Jind at 'Oakless' with her companion, the author, Bill Aitkin, the long-closed gates of the summer palace of the Maharaja of Kapurthala, Christ Church on the Mall and its tiny sister St Paul's in Landour. Mussoorie cannot be complete without a nostalgic memory of the Savoy Hotel. Fifty or sixty years ago, it was the only place to stay, to take one's lady friend and live in carefree disrespectability where sly surreptitious liaisons were as acceptable and tolerated as one's tiffin. Separated from the inevitable squalor of the squats in Mussoorie are the cemeteries at Mussoorie and Landour. Small patches of peace. Rather, like land in Dehra Dun for the living, being buried in these two cemeteries has a certain cachet, although both are pretty expensive. The graves, like the houses, closely packed together. Perhaps, some enterprising businessman will combine the two. 'Live, die and lie in the lap of Landour'.

# Touch of the Vanished Hand

Rakesh Bahadur

River Yamuna breaks out of the hills ahead of Kalsi. One moment it is swift flowing, sky-blue and green in colour, climbing and dashing against yellow-black rocks, and then, broadens in a wide expanse, flowing gently over pebbles, as if it has conquered the mountains and is now relaxed, perhaps overcome with exhaustion and displaying lassitude.

I had camped close to Kalsi, at Dakpathar, in an inspection bungalow on the banks of the river. Having reached late in the evening, there was just enough time to have a quick meal, gaze for a while on the few lights of Himachal Pradesh across the river, and smoke a pipe. Mentioning the pipe is important, since it has a bearing on the story that I am about to relate. I was carrying two pipes with my favourite tobacco. The pipes were in a leather bag, while the tobacco was in an oilskin pouch, and kept in a small moccasin bag. Needless to say, since I was camping for four days, the quantity of tobacco was sufficient for the purpose.

The night fell early, and autumn nights in the Himalayan foothills are cold. A refreshing sleep, an early morning wake-up, when the dawn was just breaking, and a good breakfast of scrambled eggs and bread; followed by two cups of hot coffee, are very conducive to start an interesting day. Although autumn days are generally clear, it was a surprise to find the sky laden with clouds promising rain.

I was going to a remote corner of the district, near its highest point, and would have to trek for about six miles. I felt that I owed myself a chance to get away from the cosmopolitan life of Dehra Dun and Mussoorie, which, interesting as it was, sometimes got on your nerves. Fortunately, no VVIPs were scheduled to arrive in Doon during the week, and one could legitimately get away from it all. In any case, the police wireless system would help me keep in touch (there were no cellular phones then). My two young daughters were staying back because something interesting, like the annual sports of the school was happening and therefore, my wife had to stay back. Of course, we had trooped over the entire district, the whole family, many times, and would have many opportunities to do so in the future. One was reasonably sure about one's tenure in the districts at that time!

The road from Kalsi rises steeply into the mountains. Because of the clouds, the mountains looked dark and forbidding. The initial few miles were gentle elevations, where the hills softly rolled in folds, but the dark clouds gave it a decidedly Moorish look, I thought. When a scenery or vision which impresses you is before the eyes, most of us believe that it will never go away, and one can recall it without effort. I have, however, learnt to disbelieve this slowly. Unless captured in a photograph or a painting, or written down on paper, the colour of the landscape as well as the timbre of the sounds associated with it, can never be recaptured. One only has a vague memory of feeling good at that time, though the mind searches vainly for what it was that made the moment special. Can you recall the gentle swoosh of the reel making an arc and then splashing in the midstream of a mountain river before the fly is taken up, or on the same bank, the lonely cry of the tern when it rises from the bushes beside the river? It was, therefore, with some amount of pleasure that I was able to place the landscape accurately on this drive.

It started to rain gently, and it only ended when I reached the inspection bungalow of my intermediate destination, about 7,000 ft high, where the metalled road also ended. It had rained here also, but the jeep track was said to be firm, and I felt that since my arrival had already been announced, it would not be proper for the trek to be put off for one day. Of course, the desire to start walking, after nearly two hours of sitting inside an ambassador car was there. And, if the surroundings at 7,000 ft were so enchanting, after an elevation of nearly fifteen hundred feet, what more would be better. As if to encourage me, some of the clouds to the north shifted, and the great snow peaks shone in their majestic glory. A quick cup of tea, and I was off.

The jeep track was tortuous, but the two petrol jeeps were in good condition, and it was around ten in the morning that I reached the small hill, from where walking was to begin. A plate of sandwiches, washed down with ice-cold water and then a cup of tea, I was ready to start. Since the provisions and my effects had been sent already, there was little luggage except for some food and tea for the way, and yes, important to reiterate, my pipes and tobacco, which I checked personally.

Lest it gives an impression that I am fond of inhaling noxious vapours all day, let me clarify that one, or at the most two, pipeful of tobacco is what I used to smoke at the time. Now, fifteen years later, weekend smoking is all that I can afford to indulge in, that too, if there is an interesting book to read, and if the phones are not ringing. How one longs for the good times when mere gusts of wind could make the phones 'dead'!

The path was moderately steep, but we set a brisk pace. There was much to admire on the way. We were climbing a ridge, with some fields on the southern slopes (since this part of the district was not really populated), while towards the north the snowy vista stretched towards me, with clouds at the roots of the peaks, having spent their moisture, and then a dense, dark jungle of mainly indigenous trees, as if, the godly peaks had decided to detach themselves from the world, the dark jungle of existence, as it were, and were floating on a bed of wispy, white clouds. Although the frost had set since it was late autumn, the heather still bloomed in patches, with bright flowers against the background of golden brown and dying bracken.

By afternoon, I had reached the inspection bungalow, set on a grassy knoll, with a deep forested valley on the north side, where a stream meandered its way, sometimes seemingly lost among the dark trees, at other places shining in the late afternoon sun. One had official business to attend to, and the sun was setting when I was done for the day. The setting sun made the peaks more interesting, the white of the snow turning to amber.

I now had a chance to examine the resthouse. Built more than one hundred years ago, it was relatively small, with one large bedroom and a sitting room, besides the normal kitchen and outhouses, situated back from the main building, but linked to it through a covered passage. The main building faced north, with a wide stone-flagged verandah, where one had the chance to sit and admire the view. As soon as the sun goes down, this part of the country becomes cool, and at this height, it was definitely cold. However, I was adequately clad, and waited till it had become dark, when the stars were starting to come out. The sitting room was very comfortable, although sparsely furnished. A log fire and something soothing from an island in the Western Isles of Scotland prepared me for dinner, which I finished early. My staff retired for the night, and I also went to the bedroom, but having finished early, decided to read for some time, sitting in a comfortable arm-chair facing the bed.

The bedroom and the sitting room both faced the verandah, and the cold necessitated the closing of the windows. One side of the bedroom led to the bathroom and on the eastern wing outside was a small patch of green, where the local *chowkidar* had made attempts to make the ground yield some beans and similar vegetables. The moonlight was strong, but after looking across the window, I drew the curtains so as to make the room cosy. Outside, the wind slowly stirred the leaves of the rhododendrons. In short, peace in this corner of the world.

The book was not very interesting, and moreover, I was not used to reading by a candle, however big it was, and I gave up the attempt. You will do well to remember, that I had not smoked my pipe even once during the day, and I now carefully filled it to the brim from the pouch, lighted it and settled to enjoy a well deserved smoke. My thoughts turned to the happenings of the day, the trek, the conversations with the villagers, and their simple expectations from the authorities. I was puzzled by one remark which the local *pradhan* had made to me separately, stating that he was surprised as to why I had chosen this particular resthouse to sleep, but I had left it at that.

I blew out the candle, and turned in for the night, going off to sleep immediately, tired after the long walk. Suddenly, I woke up after some time. Instinct made me look at my wrist-watch, which showed about two in the night. The room was in near complete darkness, but I had the feeling that I was not alone and there was someone else in the room. I thought it would have to be either a very brave or a very foolish burglar attempting to rob the district magistrate in camp. Becoming wide awake immediately, again by practice, I waited in an amused fashion for some movement on the intruder's part, but this man, whoever it was (it never occurred to me that it could be a woman) was totally silent. I began to think that perhaps, my imagination was playing tricks. I decided to sleep, yet some sixth sense stopped me. It seems surprising, but I put my head slightly high on the head-board of the bed and pulled my pillow up, the sort of position one adopts while trying to read, and which all ophthalmologists say, is bad for the eyes. There was no element of fear, and I decided to wait for whoever, or whatever it was, to make a move. My torch was besides the arm-chair, resting on a tea-table, where I had kept my pipe and the tobacco pouch, and I did not want to leave the warmth of my blankets to traipse across the room, which was fairly large. At no stage did I feel the need to challenge the visitor, perhaps secure in my own strength, and also aware of the armed guard mounted in the resthouse, as is usually the custom when the collector is in camp. I also did not feel threatened at any stage, yet my senses were alert. Nearly ten minutes later, I heard what I perceived to be a muted sigh, and then, a very soft touch, or a mere sense of something on my right hand, as if a hand just brushed me about the wrist. A touch so gentle, you'd wonder whether there was any touch at all. A slight stir of the curtain on the window in front of me, and then, a feeling that I was alone in the room again. Immediately, I felt that the presence, man or animal, real or shadow, leave the room, which became cosy once again, and I promptly fell asleep.

I am an early riser, and promptly at six in the morning, the knock announced the morning cup of tea. The sun was shining gloriously in the sky, every leaf and blade of grass looked as if it had been washed in the night, and a solitary Himalayan vulture soared in the sky, close to the snowy range in front of me. I was camping here for two nights, and despite the unusual experience of the night, did not feel it necessary to shift. I went inside to bring the pipe which was beside the ashtray near the arm-chair. The pipe was very much there, but the tobacco pouch was gone, carrying some of my best pipe tobacco. Well, it was there in the night when I had smoked, so where was it now? It had, simply and cleanly, disappeared.

My friend, the *pradhan* had a twinkle in his eyes when I met him for a cup of tea after breakfast. He asked me solicitously if I had slept well. I feigned surprise, and said that yes, I had, indeed. Out came the story that in the previous century, a party of British soldiers on a shikar trip, had camped in the resthouse for a few days. They were led by a sergeant, who died in the resthouse mysteriously, and since then, the locals avoided the building. The *chowkidar* had been here for about two years, given to drinking, and stayed in a village about a mile away. No, he saw no reason to wait after dark in the resthouse, particularly since his house was close by, and he had a cow to milk in the evening. Actually, most of these *chowkidars* do not stay in resthouses that are not frequently occupied. No district magistrate, in living memory, had halted here, and very few forest officers, too, as was evident from the visitors' book. Those who had halted were, perhaps, non-smokers as well!

I slept in the resthouse for one more night before moving back to headquarters, and was not disturbed at all. Why was I to be disturbed, considering that the tobacco had gone, perhaps, now being filled in a vintage Irish pipe. I did not regret losing the tobacco, but I did wonder whether the sergeant (if it was indeed he who had visited me), was a pipe-smoker. And, what if he smoked cigarettes, or preferred hand-rolled cigarettes. In the latter case, you would do well carry cigarette papers if you are visiting the north-west or Dehra Dun district.

I do know the question haunting (!) your mind—do I believe in ghosts? Well, I don't, and yet keep on meeting them. Not far from my house in the Kumaon Himalayas, there is the legend of a British administrator who is sometimes spotted smoking a cigarette in cold winter nights. But that is an exclusive civil service story.

# The Many Worlds of Dehra Dun

Arijit Banerji

From a quiet sleepy backwater to an aspiring with-it town with further ambitions to make it big. This is not really a history, nor even a geography, but a bunch of words to describe the growth of this quite delightful place to stay. The main background is beautiful mountain vistas, cheerful, hospitable, and welcoming people of the hills, and some climate!

We first have, with apologies, the original inhabitants who, like all original inhabitants are probably on the verge of transformation, if not inundation. They were the agricultural and orchard pioneers, basmati, *lithis*, tea gardens, and many good things from the bounty of nature. The lands and orchards, which originally belonged to retired British people, have all but disappeared as a result of a process called development. The British sold when they left, and the descendants of the original purchasers have morphed into puppies and yuppies of various hues, slowly getting lost in the beginnings of an urban sprawl, with multi-storeyed buildings taking over from the orchards.

There were, of course, the original landed gentry and their serfs about which some historian, of whom there are several in this valley, would be better qualified than the present writer to write about. Among the landed gentry were *zamindars* and maharajas who had holiday *havelis* set amongst extensive orchards and gardens in Dehra Dun and who would be citizens of the town during the season. I remember, my aunt and uncle had one such, stretching from the Bindal river to the western end of suicide alley. I remember what is now Connaught Place being sold by them when I was very small, and who knows what the selling price may have been—Rs 100 per *bigha*????

Then, we had the army, the forest department, the Survey of India, many many other government bodies and their various training establishments. These were the cream of the days of empire and several distinguished officers spent their formative and working years in the town. Before the FRI was built, the present Doon School property at Chand Bagh was the Forest College. The writer's father was at the Forest College (Chand Bagh edition) in 1925 and as a coincidence, most of the family went to the same location in its later edition. The army was, of course, the most distinguished of all the government wings, and we Doonites have always been proud of them. Distinguished to look at, distinguished by their demeanour. (I am an army buff.)

One particular form of snobbery prevalent in Dehra Dun is trying to claim an association with the town that 'goes back longer than the Jones'. The writer wins eighty percent of the time by claiming an association going back to 1925, of course, long before he was born. This form of pointless banter has frequently put the writer in a spot (twenty percent of the time) for example, when one attempt at showing off was squashed by the adversary who claimed his father had built Ghanta Ghar. Must check this out. Could not have been before 1925.

The school fraternity has always been a most important part of life in Dehra Dun, and indeed, is probably, what makes us well known throughout the land and outside. We are all proud of the many well-known institutions here and in Mussoorie, and the staff and students of all these schools are a vibrant part of our life and do us proud. Come October, and the superb Founders' Day functions lighten our life, though there are so many of them, that it becomes difficult to take them all in. If you want to know which the best institution is, I will tell you later.

We now move forward to the Partition, when the gentry of Dehra Dun used to complain for hours every day that there were too many people from a certain part of the world who were inundating and changing the (sleepy) character of the town. However, on balance who knows if this was a good thing or a bad thing (not the people but the influx). This now formed the nucleus of the puppies and yuppies, who gave us laughter, crowds, noise, shops, and similar good things of life. Two generations have passed since then and the influx has now got fully absorbed.

After the English gentry left, and the large properties and orchards were transformed, an exclusive preserve of the Brits and senior Indian gents, the Doon Club became the lamp round which the new wannabees hovered, soon to be consumed by the bright lights of their new club life. I gather, one of the newer members fired his revolver (into the air) to celebrate being consumed by the club. They had arrived.

Who else arrived?

Hordes of retired people. All shapes, sizes, ages, colours, backgrounds, careers, interests, prejudices. Some play golf, some do not play golf, some cannot play golf. Some play cards, or maybe, most play cards. Some garden, some sleep, some read, some do NGOs, some try to write, and some wonder what to do, and maybe, are still wondering. All are, of course, experts in their various fields and wait for people to ask them for free advice. Alas, as Abraham Lincoln implied, people are smart most of the time and manage to escape the offers of free advice most of the time.

You have the services retirees. Smart, clipped, distinguished. You have the government retirees. Smart, unclipped, distinguished. You have the company retirees. Smart. These worlds mingle and coalesce among much banter and jollity. The age spread here is sixty plus to ninety plus and as you, wise reader, can well imagine, this is not unlike a procession going, you know where. In the meantime, however, there is much to be done if one could only get down to doing it. If not, does it really matter?

A major problem for retirees in spending time is that there are no children here to chastise. Even youth of twenty-five think they have grown up and do not need any free advice. If they only knew. They usually live so far away in the big bad world that they need to be informed about all aspects of life away from home. The injustice of it all is compounded when they decide to inform the poor parents about how to behave in the big bad world, when to have medicine, eat, sleep, walk, (drink?). Comparing advice from various children takes up much quality time of the Dehra Dun retired population. They probably listen.

Not having become an industrial town, and unlikely to become one, the business community here are shopkeepers and traders, all getting richer by the minute, as the town grows and

India shines. They keep long working hours, but come weekends and they are off to Mussoorie, to jostle and shove on the Mall, along with hundreds of other colleagues. The fun is in crowding and jostling, eating and drinking, buying and spending, seeing and being seen, and bringing infinite joy to their brethren in Mussoorie who eagerly await these visits. Indeed, they live for them.

Then comes the season, when rich *pappays* from Meerut, Ghaziabad, Muzaffanagar, the wild west of western UP, (dare I say, Delhi), and the *jat* set in general descend on us (climb up to us?) and we all revel in how much good this does to our economy. It does not do much good, of course, to our roads, traffic, pollution, noise, litter, road rage, but at least we get to learn new sartorial trends, new behavioural norms, new and snazzy gadgets, and it gives us natives a chance to gawp at the glitz that we are missing out on. The graph grows ever onwards and upwards and this brings more and more food shops, hotels, jams, tree felling, vanishing orchards, vanishing forests, and new 'kaloneys'. The smarter visitors get taken in like the rest of us by the beauty of the valley, and buy land and buy more land. The town spreads sideways and upwards.

Then, one fine morning Dehra Dun became, from a sleepy UP backwater, the Capital. This transformed everybody into people of importance, and the emphasis shifted from what you know to who you know. This was a good thing, and gave the retirees and everybody else much more to talk about. Traffic took on a glitter that it never had. Cars with blue flashers, red flashers, (which are higher in the heirarchy?) beacons, sirens, uniformed policemen pushing cars and citizens out of the way, and important looking people looking important sitting in their cars. From the length of the processions and the amount of noise generated, one

could estimate whether the main occupant of the main car (one person) was equivalent to the Emperor Shah Jahan or a lesser mortal. This must surely have influenced his son, the Emperor Aurangzeb, to take a greater interest in Dehra Dun and thus remembered to send Guru Ram Rai here to start a settlement.

In any case, what was always evident in these cavalcades was the urgency with which they had to zoom. Uttarakhand being a border state, there is always the chance of an emergency, an invasion, or an infiltration, which makes it essential in the national interest to go as fast as you can, whether you are going towards the problem or running away from it. There is an added blessing here—the public get to see many policemen even though they are only guarding the cavalcades, glaring at everybody, and not catching criminals. That is a different department.

Though our little city has grown to the point where Skoda Octavias and Hyundai Sonatas are passe, and one sees Mercedes, Audi, and BMW on the roads, the King of the Road remains the caparisoned white Ambassador, with red and blue flashers and ear-piercing sound effects. It could be the inspector of animal husbandry rushing to Haridwar to check if the cows have been properly inseminated, or a similar problem of urgent national importance.

Having said all this, the presence of government was a blessing to anyone who had problems, and one did not need to go to Lucknow or other places to solve them. It is a moot point whether their presence created other problems—the jury is out on this. But roads, power supply, telephone connections improved and land prices zoomed up faster than the VIP cavalcades. This zooming continues, which has brought another class of people here—persons of wealth (and eminence?) who buy land either to build and live or not build and keep. This is, of course, a blessing for all the locals, but not much of a blessing for ordinary people with aspirations to live in Dehra Dun.

All these worlds or their equivalents obviously exist in all cities, but in the bigger cities one tends to live in one's own chosen little world with nary a thought for the rest. Since Dehra Dun is anything but large, all these worlds are in close proximity, and mesh and move and mingle more than in most other places. There is little social climbing in a big city sense because there are really no great social heights to climb, but our residents do indulge themselves in trying to move around these various worlds to see if any of them offers any chances of climbing. Alas! the answer is usually no.

For a town as small as Dehra Dun we have a large number of NGOs but here again, alas, the major component of membership seems to be retired people, sometimes up to the age of eighty and beyond. This leaves us woefully short of actual field workers for the average NGO, and we have to suffer from the syndrome of too many chiefs and not enough Indians. In spite of this, a lot of good work is done. For example, the Rajaji National Park has been practically cleared of human habitation and a very effective rehabilitation programme put into effect by the joint efforts of Government and NGOs. The regeneration of the forests in the park, the increased green cover after lopping stopped, and the removal of pressure on forest grasslands from the thousands of erstwhile residents' cattle have all contributed to a rebirth of the park, an increase in wildlife, including the tiger. There are many other examples of NGOs contributing to the improvement of our lives.

It is, probably, not known that the Rajaji National Park is the northern-most range of the Asian elephant. Encroachment into forests and the spread of habitation took away the elephants' natural habitat, leaving the animals no choice, but to stray into human settlements which led to conflict. By humans intruding into their traditional range, the elephants were left with no alternative but to try and cross the main railway line that runs through their reserve, resulting in tragic cases of elephants being run over by speeding trains. Concerted action by citizens, government, and railways seems to have reduced this tragic problem.

A special attraction of Dehra Dun was the abundance of bird life and wildlife within the limits of the extended town. With the rapid spread of the town, we see less and less of our former companions. The more's the pity. There is no answer to this unfortunate result of progress and urbanisation, but spare a thought for the thousands of animals, whose habitat we have taken away. Nocturnal visits by leopards were quite frequent in the outskirts of the town some years ago but have become very rare of late. *Jungli murghi* were sighted very often, but as the days go by, this is becoming less and less often. One still sees hares at night and we hope these gentle creatures are not destroyed by our progress.

Dehra Dun has always had good eating houses, starting with Kwality which was born in Dehra Dun, and good bakeries and confectioners. This tradition continues with the old eating houses maintaining their standards and new eating house constantly coming up. Nirula's is ever popular, and McDonalds is a recent entrant. With the growing tourist trade, industrialisation, new educational institutions, new hotels, and the exodus away from the crowded dusty plains to our Dehra in the Dun, the town grows. It is our job to see it improves as well.

Not easy, but so far there is a lot to be said for Dehra Dun (rhymes with fun).

# How Green was my Valley?
## [Wildlife and Forests of Dehra Dun]

Bikram Grewal

The Dehra Dun Valley is cradled between two mighty mountain ranges: the west Himalayas in the north and the Shivalik range running parallel in the south. To the west it is bordered by the holy river Yamuna, and to the east by the even more hallowed Ganga, on whose banks rest the sacred cities of Rishikesh and Haridwar. Perennial streams like the Asan, Suswa, Tons, Song and the Jakhan water the valley, turning it into a verdant carpet of green. Half of the valley is covered by pure and mixed forests dominated by the soaring sal tree (*Shorea robusta*). The rest is a mix of cultivated agricultural land, agro-forestry plantations, old tea gardens, orchards, urbanised areas, cantonments and riverine scrubland. The British hill station of Mussoorie looks down imperiously on the forests below.

It is, therefore, appropriate that the British should decide to set up the Forest Research Institute in this lush valley. Established as the Imperial Forest Research Institute in 1906, it was located in Chand Bagh, where the elite Doon School is now located. But the institute ran out of space and had to be moved a few kilometres down where its new building was inaugurated in 1929. This glorious Greco-Roman building was designed by the architect, C.G. Blomfield and built by Sardar Ranjit Singh, a contractor who also built Lutyen's Delhi. To me, it is the finest building in India, even more magnificent than the Rashtrapati Bhavan in the capital. Spread over hundreds of acres, it houses a charming botanical garden and five museums.

Another important institution in Dehra Dun is the Wildlife Institute at Chandrabani. Set up in 1982 and given autonomy in 1986, it has produced some of the finest research in the field of environment. Today, it is the conscious keeper of the environmental movement, often correcting and exposing wrong-doing by the state forest departments, like the fudging of tiger census figures.

Dehra Dun has had a close call. In the early Sixties, the hills were scarred by the greed of the limestone quarry mafia. This coterie of well-connected and powerful people managed to obtain licenses to extract the lucrative limestone. The hillsides reverberated with the sound of dynamite, causing havoc to the land, the wildlife and the inhabitants. The natural limestone aquifers were close to extinction. A growing concern among the residents led them to approach the Supreme Court and, after a bitter fight that went on for five long years, the court ordered the closure of these mines. Aided by the abundant rain that the valley is blessed with, the scarred hillsides slowly regained their pristine look.

But now, there's a new threat. The city has been declared the capital of the newly-formed state of Uttaranchal (now, Uttarakhand), a decision that has accelerated the crass urbanisation. The city is expanding and creeping into the pristine forests.

It was during the glorious green days of the Nineties, after the mining ban and before the urbanisation, that I decided to become a part-time resident of Dehra Dun. It was a sleepy town with *litchi* orchards and fields of basmati rice and people lived in old bungalows. Dalanwala was not the slum it is now. There were no supermarkets and no night clubs. Life was gentle, and the pace languorous. I bought a quaint house near the Malsi Deer Park and started a love affair which over the years has been endured. Soon, Malsi became too crowded and I moved further and deeper into the forest, and acquired a hillside on the river Tons. This is where I plan to finally hang my boots and await the call.

After a misspent life chasing and writing about birds, I thought I would start a quiet study of the birds that inhabit the valley. It was a tough act to follow, for my predecessors included the venerable B.B. Omaston who first published an article entitled 'Birds nesting in the Tons Valley' as early as 1897, and continued doing so till the publication of his definitive 'Birds of Dehra Dun and the adjacent Hills' in 1935. There were others like J. George and M.D. Wright who continued to contribute to the study of the valley's avi-fauna. The mantle has now fallen on the young but competent shoulders of Dhananjai Mohan and A.P. Singh.

The valley is a birder's paradise for it covers a variety of habitats, and this is reflected in the very impressive checklist of more than four hundred birds, including twenty-three 'globally threatened' avian species. If you include the surrounding hills the

count crosses a staggering six hundred. One day, in my garden on the Tons, Bill Harvey, Nikhil Devasar and I were ringing some birds and found a strange and unfamiliar looking small bird which was clearly a member of the Wren-babbler family. We consulted all the available literature and to our immense joy, it turned out to be a Nepal Wren-babbler, a bird only recently discovered by science and hitherto thought to be endemic to Nepal.

A spot that never fails to surprise me is this marvellous waterbody called the Asan Barrage near the sanctified town of Paonta Sahib. In recent years, it has come up with such rarities as the Falcated Duck and the Black-necked Grebe, not to mention Penduline Tits. Now, the tourism department in its wisdom wants to convert these marshlands into a water-sports complex. I feel sorry for the lone breeding pair of Pallas' Fish Eagle that has nested in the same Semul tree for as long as I can remember. A short drive from here lies Karvapani (literally, 'bitter water'), a magnificent stretch of dense and high sal forest, which covers the northern aspect to the Shivalik hills, stretching from Asarori, Malhan through to Timli. The charming forest resthouse was converted into a temporary jail during the infamous emergency in 1975. The temple of Manak Sidh stands close-by.

Another great stretch of forest and a personal favourite is the Thano forest, which is continuous with the Garhwal hills and connected to the Panduwal–Lachiwala forest in the south. It's a superb spot for observing altitudinal migrants. The river Song and its attendant marshes are great for kingfishers and the occasional Black Stork. The Kalu Sidh Temple is a bonus. Unfortunately, Lachiwala has been converted into a picnic spot and hordes of tourists converge to frolic in the river.

Other forest blocks such as Barkot, Jhajra and Majaun, too, are under threat from the ever-increasing hunger for land. Be it the timbre mafia, the developers building new homes or the industrialists keen to exploit the tax benefits offered by the government, they are all on the prowl, grabbing what they can and destroying as soon as they possibly can. If this goes on unchecked, the Doon Valley will soon become a polluted wilderness.

Perhaps, the greatest tragedy is the story of the Rajaji National Park, a large part of which actually lies in the valley, especially the forty kilometre strech from Phanduwala, through to Kansrao and ending up at Motichur. The Chilla block lies across the river Ganga. Fossils excavated in the Shivalik hills show the remains of prehistoric elephants like the *Stegodon ganesa*, whose tusks were ten feet long.

Today, their 'lesser' descendants find refuge in this park. Their sanctuary is a fragile asylum, surrounded as it is by the three burgeoning cities of Dehra Dun, Rishikesh and Haridwar. Over 2,000 families, with their 15,000 cattle, live within and in the immediate vicinity of the park, criss-crossed by railway lines, roads and canals. The ecologically vital Chilla–Motichur corridor has been blocked by intense human activity and development, not to mention an army ammunition dump, several villages, the Delhi–Dehra Dun railway line, the Haridwar–Dehra Dun highway and the Chilla power channel. However, conservation of this corridor is not impossible if it gets legal protection. Land for rehabilitation of the village has been identified and funds earmarked for a flyover between Raiwala and Haridwar near Motichur to enable elephants to pass safely beneath.

Van Gujjars are a nomadic Muslim tribe that has been living in Rajaji for several years. They claim that they first came to the Terai as part of the dowry of a Kashmir princess. The Gujjars are nomadic graziers who move their herd to the upper Himalayas in summer, giving the forests a chance to rejuvenate in their six-month absence. However, over the years, loss of traditional pastoral land has forced them to make Rajaji their permanent home, putting immense biotic pressure on the park. It is not unusual to see these nomads whiz through the park on noisy motorcycles carrying milk cans.

Following a Supreme Court order to rehabilitate the Gujjars from the designated protected area, efforts were made to relocate them. The painful procedure began in 2002 and after a traumatic year, 193 Gujjar families were resettled to a village, Gaindikhatta. But several thousand Van Gujjars continue to live within the sanctuary. The Chilla block was recently cleared of all Van Gujjars and almost immediately a camera trap set up by the members of the Wildlife Institute recorded a pregnant tigress—the first breeding record in over twenty years. Different matter, she was later killed by poachers.

The elephant–man conflict is far from being resolved. Man is eating into their land, forcing these gentle giants into the open where they are persecuted, chased and shot at. But there is hope. In the past, there were instances of elephants being run over by speeding trains, especially in the Kansrao area. It took several years to get the railway authorities to agree to reduce the speed of trains passing through this belt. As a result, not a single elephant has been killed since 2000.

I have spent many happy hours in Rajaji, driving through unknown corners of the park, entering through all its gates. I have stayed in the forest resthouses in Dholkhand, Beribarra, Kansrao and Motichur. I have seen Yellow-throated Martins chase and kill Kalij Pheasants. I have seen a King Cobra slither away and observed a leopard stalk a barking deer. I've been chased innumerable times by irate elephants. It's a lovely forest. And, I can only pray it stays the way it is.

# Doon: Up Close and Personal

Nayantara Sahgal

My coffee has the earthy scent and flavour of the clay *kulhar* I am using instead of a china mug. A Mexican friend taught me to drink it in earthenware and, like tea, it tastes richest this way. I make an early morning ritual of it on the verandah where a luxuriously sal-forested hillside spreads high and wide on my left and slopes steeply down to the boulder-strewn riverbed beneath my garden wall. The dry bed becomes the rushing Bindal river during the monsoon when rain floods the hillside and mist shrouds the garden. But come September, cloud, mist and mystery vanish along with the river as if they had never been.

At this hour, the sun's just risen rays barely brush the sal treetops but the whole forest will be sunlit by the time I finish my coffee. Facing me, the northern hill ranges south-east to Garhwal. Morning light will lay bare the bald bleached patches on it, left by rapacious limestone quarrying. Though the Supreme Court stopped the quarrying, scars have an uncanny durability, reminding me that Dehra Dun once meant a jail where my father[1] and my uncle[2] were imprisoned together during one phase of the fight for freedom. The cold cement of the jail offices in Allahabad, Lucknow, Bareilly and Almora, besides Dehra Dun, the grate of rusted iron padlocks, the anguish of saying goodbye to my three parents again and again, hands clinging through unbreakable iron bars, are enduring childhood memories.

Before we made our home here in 1985, Nirmal Mangat Rai and I used to drive up from Delhi on visits to my mother[3], who had come to live here in 1970 after resigning her seat in Parliament. Why did you choose Derha Dun, people asked her, expecting her to say she had chosen the site for its view, the place for its climate and natural beauty, and hearing her say instead that she had an emotional connection with its jail and a nostalgia for her first political assignment. In 1937, she had become the world's first woman cabinet minister and had covered the hills and plains of Uttar Pradesh for the next two years as minister for health and local self-government in Gobind Ballabh Pant's cabinet.

The house she built, with its gift of hillside and its extravaganza of space and sky and stars, was only a hundred and fifty miles from Delhi, but a world removed from the corridors of power and the atmosphere of jostling ambition which is peculiar to capital cities. In Delhi—recently divorced, hard up, and (for reasons I have recounted elsewhere) living in

[1]Ranjit Sitaram Pandit
[2]Jawaharlal Nehru
[3]Vijaya Lakshmi Pandit

sin—I struggled to make a living out of journalism, at a time when writing did not pay and political analysis was a male monopoly. I broke through that male bastion to hammer out political commentary in a long relationship with the *Indian Express*, fanning out to other newspapers and magazines. It was for me the beginning of an impassioned involvement with what India stood for and how she should be governed. In Dehra Dun, far from the din of battle, I sat under a blossom-laden cassia tree on the lawn while the story called 'Crucify Me' wrote itself, and then another called 'Earthly Love', so easily did one shift into another frame of mind that gave imagination free rein.

Upper Rajpur Road was truly isolated in those days. My mother had no neighbour on either side. *Jungli murghi* strutted along the garden's low stone parapet. Once, a deer came calling. One night, a leopard left a flurry of chicken feathers on the lawn. Nirmal and I took walks along the rocky river-bed, or across the bridge toward Sahastradhara, or along the Eastern Canal that carried the Rispana river's waters to the town's homes and gardens and had at one time served the tea estates that had flourished in Dehra Dun. We spent evenings on the moon-drenched verandah facing Mussoorie's hilltop lights, drinking illegal whisky during prohibition. We did our shopping in Rajpur bazaar, a twenty-minute walk up the road, where Ashraf the barber gave Nirmal a periodic haircut. We ate *samosas* and *jalebis* at the Sardarji's popular teashop, made friends with the postmaster, and discovered a community of Hindus, Muslims, Christians and Buddists—Indians and Tibetans—who lived up the slope from the bazaar and had known each other over a generation or two. This harmonious mix gave no indication of the religion-mania that was to destroy a historic mosque in this very state in a few years' time. Nor,

did this quiet enclave, or Dehra Dun itself, succumb to the long-lasting repercussions of this barbaric event. We came to the conclusion that different kinds of people, practising different customs, worshipping different gods, and celebrating their differences together, are the surest guarantee against racial or religious madness and the claim to exclusiveness that produces it. An individual who is locked up all his life in a cell without light or air will go mad and die. Exactly so do cultures decay and civilisations disappear. The magic of renewal and regeneration is brought about by the stranger who crosses our path, the 'other' who is not in the least like us, and for that reason can breathe new life into our bloodstream. India has long understood this wisdom and prospered by it, acknowledging her debt to strangers through all her centuries.

The only nuisance I recall during our visits was the blast of a loudspeaker at the crack of dawn from an ashram down the road. I walked down to investigate, expecting to find a congregation praying at the top of its combined lungs but the compound was deserted. I banged on a side door. It was opened by an angry fat-bellied man who must have had to get up from his *charpai* in the bare room to answer my knock. I guessed that, lying prone on his *charpai*, all he had to do was stretch out one finger to switch the canned *bhajans* on or off, probably in mid-snore, without disturbing his sleep. Hitler had famously used this economical technique at his rallies, shutting off the ecstatic hysteria of his Nazi legions with a tiny flick of his wrist. The fat man and I exchanged furious words. The noise shrieked on, until I complained to the district magistrate who took action. Some years later, our area lost the sanctity of silence along with its cleanliness when a temple was built and a bazaar and shops and fast food came up around it. So did noise, brisk commerce, beggars and mounting garbage. We came to another conclusion. Worship is a matter of the heart, not of lungpower, and religion, like love, is a private affair. Make it in public, use it to goad and incite, tack it to a political agenda, and it becomes an obscenity.

My mother asked me if I would like to settle in Dehra Dun. I put off decision, fearing I would miss the intellectual sparkle and crackle of Delhi. And then, it seemed, decision would have to wait. In 1979, the Janta government appointed me Ambassador to Italy. Nirmal decreed we must marry since an Ambassador of India could not be half of an unwed couple, so we got married. The government tottered. Then it fell, and the new government axed the appointment. I let Dehra Dun wait and took the opportunity of two fellowships in the United States to write two novels. Not every woman has the good fortune to marry a feminist who will reverse roles to shop, cook and clean while his wife gets on with her time-bound novel. So, we did not move to the Doon until 1985 and in recognition of our independent identities we put both our nameplates at the gate. This seemed all the more necessary when the 'hindu *nari*' image overtook films and TV.

I had spent enchanted childhood summers in the pine forests of my father's estate near Almora where he grew fruit and flowers, experimented with wheat, set up a village school, bee-hives and a tannery, and named this paradise 'Ritusamhara' after the Kalidasa poem he later translated from Sanskrit into English. Congress workers held summer camps at 'Ritusamhara'. Friends of the family came to visit, among them, Boshi and Gertrude Sen, add the American artist Earl Brewster with his wife, all of whom had made Almora their home. I did not come across the awesome grandeur of Garhwal's interior until August

1988. The last stop on the road journey I made with friends was Gaurikund, from where I joined straggling lines of humanity to walk fourteen kilometres uphill from Gaurikund to Kedarnath, accompanied by the Mandakini all the way. The climb to nearly 12,000 feet took me seven hours and at the temple, I did what I had never been impelled to do before, offer a puja. Perhaps, it was the lean quiet setting of the temple—so unlike the commotion around Badrinath—which legend had it was built by the Pandavas. Perhaps, it was the sag of pilgrimage: the unending procession of men and women I had passed at every turn, toiling up or making their sodden way down the mountain, some barefoot, through ankle-deep slush on that day of incessant rain.

Four years ago, when life-after-Nirmal began, I embarked on it with the caution of an invalid learning to walk again, doubting that I ever would. Dehra Dun had meanwhile, become the capital of a new state and was caught up in the throes of transformation, with all the growing pains that accompany change. Empty space was fast disappearing and hedges had become history as houses sprang up along upper Rajpur Road, barricaded behind high iron-spiked walls, and more houses behind them. There were sentry boxes, night watchmen, burglaries—one in my own house—and spectacular car crashes as traffic grew too big for roads and ignored rules. In town glass-fronted shops sold imported brands from shoes to virgin olive oil, eyelashes, lotions and potions at globalised prices. Huge, new, heavily guarded jewellery stores, some specialising in diamonds, arrived in glittering profusion. I hoped that olives at least—or some equivalent benefit—if not diamonds, would reach the mountains whose people had fought for statehood and the better life they believed it would bring them. I also hoped that with health, beauty, and the fountain of youth ours for the taking in the Himalayan herbs growing wild on our hills, Uttarakhand would patent and profit by this abundant miraculous yield before some foreign brand did.

Two additions to the new state were a matter for pride. One is the Centre for Tibetan and Himalayan Studies in Sahastradhara with its magnificent Songtsen Library, just fifteen minutes' drive from my house. It was opened by the Dalai Lama is 2003 and like all the Buddhist institution, I have seen it is immaculately maintained and inviolably serene. The other is Yog-Ganga at the top of Rajpur bazaar where two inspired students of B.K.S. Iyengar carry on the priceless tradition of hatha-yoga. But this is not one more school of hatha-yoga. Here, the laziest and most reluctant anatomies are trained to perform *asanas* of mathematical precision and perfection using a variety of props that distinguish the Iyengar school of yoga from other schools. Both the Tibetan Centre and Yog-Ganga attract scholars and students from all over the world and are reason enough for the Doon to be on the world map.

It took me longer to catch up with the community of 'outsiders' from other states and other countries now resident in Dehra Dun—the influx of strangers with whom every society needs to renew and revitalise itself. Different subjects entered conversation. Food and drink became more enjoyable. I found that learning to walk again was not an insurmountable problem.

There are still reassuring reminders that some things need not change: roasted coffee beans from Paltan bazaar, freshly baked brown bread, *puri–tarkari*, and the comfort of beautifully stocked bookshops where every request is met and fulfilled with a most unbusinesslike affection. My hillside is still here, too, still thickly wooded, I hope for all time.

# The Net and Nostalgia

Ramachandra Guha

A friend of mine complains that I am somewhat opportunistic about my use of the term 'home town'. Depending on the context, and my own interest, I use either the town I was born and reared, or the city where my forefathers came from and to which I have since returned. I plead guilty to unprincipled opportunism, but also to an honest confusion. Just as some men have two wives and other men have two nationalities, I have two home towns. Why must I choose between one and the other?

My conscious memories of Bangalore/Bengaluru go back to the year 1962. For the next thirty years, I visited the place once a year, sometimes twice, staying for a few weeks or a few months each time. Since 1994, it has been my permanent and full-time *home*. Still, although I think of it seldom, in my dreams my other (and original) home town pops up every so often. Its

dense and crowded bazaar figures, but more often I dream of the valley in which the town is set: of its pine forests, its swift-running streams, its views of the hills, and its birds beautiful and grand, from the Paradise Flycatcher to the Red-billed Blue Magpie.

Recently, however, the town and the valley have come to occupy my waking hours as well. This is because I have been asked to contribute to a new website devoted to its favourite sport, football.

The Indian city with which football is generally associated is, of course, Kolkata. As it happens, one of Kolkata's best-loved footballers was a man from Dehra Dun. His name was Ram Bahadur, who—most unusually for a mercenary on the Maidan—played for one club alone, East Bengal. As a thrusting half-back, he helped his club to several league titles, and to several IFA Shields and Durand Cups. He was capped many times for India, playing in the Rome Olympics of 1960 and in the gold-medal winning team at the Bangkok Asian Games in 1962.

I knew Ram Bahadur intimately, for he was my uncle's closest friend. I have written of him and their friendship elsewhere (see, www.dehradunfootball.com) but here I want to write of a Dehra Dun footballer who played for East Bengal even before Ramu *dai* did; in fact, who introduced the younger man to the club. His name was Bir Bahadur, and like his protégé, he went on to be capped for India. As a 'roving centre-half', he played in the 1958 Asian Games, before the shift to a 4–2–4 system saw him losing his place in the national side.

On retiring from football Biru *dai* returned to the valley, and took up a job in the school where I studied. Unusually, for a man of his class and profession, he both spoke immaculate English and did not put on an ounce of flesh after his playing career had ended. He occasionally appeared in staff versus student matches, his elegant through-passes—invariably muffed up by a puffing old schoolmaster—revealing glimpses of the player he once was. In those days I was even more crazy about football than cricket. So, when I had a free evening I would take myself off to Bir Bahadur's apartment, where he would brew me a cup of tea and tell me stories of his days in the game.

Bir Bahadur had played football in the decade when the Indian football team was not merely a joke, when it won at the Asian Games and came a creditable fourth in the Olympics. He would speak with affection of the men he had played with and against, such as Sailen Manna of Bengal, Neville D'Souza of Bombay, Peter Thangaraj of Madras, and—his particular hero—the giant Kempiah of Bangalore. Biru *dai* was a deeply modest man, who rarely spoke of his own prowess or achievements. He did however, tell me one story about himself, whose lessons go far beyond the sporting field. The story went like this:

Dehra Dun was once part of the great Gurkha kingdom, and the Nepali-speakers who stayed on in the valley, were the males, and regarded the army as their career of choice. When Bir Bahadur turned eighteen, he enlisted as a jawan. He learnt (I suppose) how to carry and load a rifle, but most of his time was spent on the football field. In those days, his preferred position was on the right-wing, and it was in that capacity that he was capped for the services. Soon after he joined the army, he found himself playing in the semi-final of the Santosh Trophy (against the railways, if memory serves me right). The first part of the match went very well. One of Biru's crosses was headed into goal, and then he himself cut in and scored from about twenty yards out. Services were two–nil up, a quarter-of-an-hour into the game. Just before half-time, they earned a penalty, and the captain summoned the eager young winger to take the strike. Biru ran in and shot hard, but the ball hit the post and rebounded safely into play.

It should have been 3–0 at the whistle. Instead, after play recommenced the railways managed to get in two goals, the match went into extra-time, and eventually the services lost. In the space of two hours, the young man had come face-to-face with Kipling's imposters in full and equal measure. From this cruel experience he drew the lesson that it was better to be safe than sorry. So, he left the wing and became a half-back instead.

From school in the valley I went on to college in Delhi. By now cricket had become my favourite sport, but I still loved football enough to be a fixture at the Ambedkar Stadium for the DCM and Durand Championships. I normally supported East Bengal, for they had Shyam Thapa as their star forward, except when they played Mafatlal, for whom not one, not two, but as many as three Dehra Dun footballers were then playing. Two were regulars—Amar Bahadur and Ranjit Thapa. A third had his best years behind him, and so came on only when things were really desperate. This was Bhupinder Singh Rawat, known to his fellow-townsmen as 'Bhupi', but to the Delhi crowd as 'Scooter' or, more accurately, 'Sc-o-o-o-t-a-r-r-r-r', allegedly because his scurrying small steps brought that mode of transport to mind.

Bhupi Rawat was a member of the legendary Gurkha Brigade team that won the Durand Cup in 1967 and 1968. He had then moved on to better things—and certainly better pay—with Mafatlal. The string of trophies which that club won in the early 1970s owed much to Rawat and his *pahari* compatriots. But by the end of the decade he was playing, as it were, from memory. I have an abiding recollection of a match played in my last year at university—1978–9—when Mafatlal and East Bengal were locked at one-all with about ten minutes to play. Bhupi came on as a substitute, to cheers of 'Scootaarr!'. Within a minute or two—I am not making this up—his team was awarded a penalty. Prudence would have dictated Ranjit or Amar taking the kick, but sentiment and fear made the captain ask Bhupi to do the job instead, although he had not touched the ball in the match, nor very much in previous matches either.

Bhupi Rawat placed the ball on the spot, and slowly retreated twenty yards. He took a deep breath, possibly two or three, and ran in terrier-like, at great speed and in very many little steps. When he got there he let fly. The ball hit the cross-bar with such terrific power that—I *swear* I am not making this up—the piece of sturdy and well-seasoned wood shook fearfully for a full five minutes afterwards. However, instead of finding the back of the net the ball came back into play. The end of the story is foretold—East Bengal went on to win in extra-time.

The internet is regarded as the very embodiment of a 'cutting-edge' technology, but—as doubtless others have also found out—this superb illustration of man's capacity to look forward also sometimes aids him in looking backward. For my part, I am grateful to this new site for returning me to my beloved valley, for stoking memories which—these being *human* memories, after all—are sometimes sticky and at other times sweet.

# Life and Times of the Savoy

Ganesh Saili

When I first met Anand Jauhar (better known as 'Nandu' to his friends) in the early 1980s he had finally come home to his roots in Mussoorie, having spent his youth running an Indian restaurant in London's Marble Arch. Little did any of us, my friends and I, have an inkling then that a chance meeting would for two decades and more, change our lives forever. Nothing was ever to be the same again. For, be it summer or winter, the old Savoy was a great watering-hole. This was where author Ruskin Bond and I, met a whole gamut of characters: film stars, rogues, politicians, business tycoons, fly-by-night operators and some fast fading beauty queens.

Of course, you could still find their flourishes in the visitors' book. I last saw it on the front desk, to the left of Chatter Singh Negi, an old employee in his eighties (when he retired three years ago, it was rumoured that he had gone through two wives and seventy years in the hotel). Between its green-and-gold covers was a veritable *Who's Who* of Mussoorie's early history: His Holiness the Dalai Lama and Panchem Lama, Haile Selassie, the Emperor of Ethiopia, Prince Norodum Sihanouk and even the Nehrus—from Motilal, Jawaharlal, Indira and down to Rajiv. All guests at the hotel could waken at dawn to see from their window, the long line of Himalayas spanning the horizon to the north, and to watch the peaks catch fire, one after another, as the sun came up. While lower down to the south stretched the Doon Valley enshrouded in haze, where the winter line showed up so clearly, a blue haze where the line joined the sky it was brilliant red.

In the 1960s, if you could not find a room at the Savoy, you had a choice between the imperial Charleville Hotel in Happy Valley, which turned into the National Academy of Administration; followed by the Hakman's Grand Hotel, in the middle of the Mall Road, which lamentably has gone to seed and the Stiffles, briefly reincarnated as a roller-skating rink, caught fire and was reduced to ashes. The Savoy, like a lost tusker, in a changing world, stumbled on.

Like other sprawling hotels, this too once had a life of its own. There were rich patrons; usually the ex-rulers and landed gentry who, with their retinues, occupied whole wings of the hotel. After them came the civil and military officers on furlough who partied the day away. On my first visit, I found a whiff of the era still lingering in the air. Breakfast, lunches and dinners were served with personal attention to individual tastes. There was nightly dancing in the ballroom. Cabaret artists of varied backgrounds chased the night away with their repertoire of song, dance and striptease. There was frolic and fun: lawn tennis and squash; snooker and skittles; card tables and chess games and fancy dress balls. Close by was the Library to satisfy the guests' fondness for reading.

The only constant in a sea of visitors, was the hotel staff. It had a firm pecking order, a sort of totem pole, if you like, starting from the manager, down to the stewards, reception counter clerks, chefs, waiters, down to the night *chowkidar*, the room boys, and the sweepers—each one claimed to be privy to some secret or the other.

Often, Nandu too, would get caught up in a game. He had his own plans for a grand future. We discovered this when he got it into his head to christen the old Savoy bar. After all, what was a bar without a name? It had dawned upon him after a visit to the historic Raffles Hotel in Singapore, where he had seen the Writers' Bar. Brass plaques on the walls proclaimed that Somerset Maugham had been there, as had Conrad and Graham Greene. One day, he asked us why couldn't the Savoy too, have its very own *Writers' Bar.*

'Writers' Bar! Where on earth would you get writers from?' I asked.

'Well! Just for starters *you* are here! Aren't you a writer, Ruskin Bond?' he exclaimed in triumph, adding: 'Don't you know some other writer types, Ruskin?'

'None! I'm afraid...the Fitzgerald's *Lost Weekend* variety is out of fashion!' exclaimed Ruskin. 'Why not just call it the Horizontal Bar instead?'

But Nandu would have none of it. He gave us a withering look, careening on: 'They don't have to be the heavy boozer types only!'

Who could argue with that?

Finally, after much dithering and tippling, Ruskin and I simply capitulated. After all, a hotel with a hundred years of history behind it, there was no telling who could *not* have dropped by for a drink even if it were just plain *nimbu-paani!* Soon, the deed was done. Over the weekend, the plaques were made in wood by the local coffin-maker and hammered on to the walls. They celebrate the often tenuous link with writers like John Lang, the Australian-born novelist (in the 1850s, he could possibly have been a judge at the old Mussoorie School Inter-House Debate! Who's to tell!); Jim Corbett, the *shikari*-turned naturalist (whose parents married in Mussoorie); John Masters who spent time with the Gurkhas in the Doon; and even Pearl S. Buck the Nobel laureate, though she never wrote a word about our hill station! But she did stay at the hotel.

Though it was not writers only who strayed into the old Savoy. To appreciate what the hotel was all about, you will have to travel back in time, and get a feel of the origins of the hill station. As they say in fairy tales, once upon a time, Mussoorie too was 'the queen of resorts and the resort of kings', a sort of meeting place for the rich and the powerful. But the town was never really anything officious or stuffy. It was where you could find yourself sailing into a 'fishing-fleet' of young girls looking for eligible bachelors, or meet rakish bachelors whispering sweet nothings into the ears of 'grass widows' under the eaves. And if you think, the husbands had run away or were absconding, you're wrong! Poor things thought they had better things to do—like minding the affairs of the State in an Indian summer in the sultry plains! Mussoorie was, and to a limited extent, still is, a place where you can let your hair down without inviting social censure.

With the passage of times, the need arose for a place of quiet luxury. Cecil D. Lincoln, a barrister from Lucknow, took over the lands of the old Mussoorie School, pulled down the school and built a hotel in its stead, naming it after the Fayrest Manor in Europe. To his credit goes the English Gothic architecture, its fine proportions, its lancet-shaped narrow windows along the corridors and the verandahs. You can still find the original school emblem, a four-leafed clover, peeping out from amongst the eaves.

Two simple spires, without any parapet, surmount the corners of the main building—rearing their heads in pride constituting the main façade. If you consider the fact that the first motor car came to the hill station in 1920, you can only admire the sheer ingenuity and dogged perseverance of the early settlers. Men and material came up the bridle path from Rajpur. Everything came up this winding serpentine trail by bullock cart. Massive Victorian and Edwardian furniture, billiard tables, grand pianos, Burmese teak for the ballroom floors, rotund barrels of beer and cases of champagne and cognac—all the requirements of a fine hotel trundled up the hill on lumbering bullock carts.

Launched in 1902, the hotel was—'like a phoenix rising from the ashes of a school' gushed a local scribe. Royalty trooped to town when four years later, Her Royal Highness, the Princess of Wales—later, Queen Mary—attended a garden party in the Savoy grounds. No soon had she left, a severe earthquake hit Mussoorie. Many buildings were flattened and the hotel had to be closed for an year. But by 1907, it was up and about and ready to go.

In between the two Great Wars, in the 'gay Twenties', Mussoorie entered its days of wine and roses. In its heydays, the Savoy orchestra played every night, and the ballroom was full of couples dancing the night away. You could do the fox trot or waltz to the happy numbers or do your own thing.

On a visit in 1926, Lowell Thomas, in *The Land of the Black Pagoda* wrote: 'There is a hotel in Mussoorie where they ring a bell just before dawn so that the pious may say their prayers and the impious get back to their own beds.'

When I asked Nandu, he confirmed: 'We employed an old, short-sighted *chowkidar* to ring the separation bell at four every morning.... It guaranteed absolute privacy to the guests!'

During the Second World War, the British and the American military officers on leave, sought amusement in the hills and flocked to the place. Legend has us believe that the sale of whisky used to be so high that Lincoln would have all the empty bottles from the previous day's sale, collected and brought down to the cellar. Gently, he would coax every last drop of scotch from each bottle. Miraculously, he would have two full bottles ready for house guests the next day!

It was not about tippling alone. Sometimes, guests would be staggered by the size of the luxury suites. I was told that one day, when the hotel was full, an elderly couple was shown the bridal suite. 'What will we do with this?' the old man exclaimed. 'Sir! If you're shown the ballroom, you don't *have to* dance!' said the ever-resourceful Negi.

Anand Jauhar's father holidaying in the hills bought the complex in 1946. Till just three years ago, it was still a family-run hotel; when due to a bout of ill-health, Nandu gave up his shares to the new owners. What's happening now? We are often asked. Well! They are trying to update it with some modern-day creature comforts, without changing the character of this fine heritage hotel. One wishes them luck in their endeavours!

On my last visit here, as I finished taking pictures, I bid farewell to the charming old billiards room, (where in 1900, a leopard was found hiding under the rosewood table) I try to catch some of the spirit of the heydays of the Raj. I remind myself that the history of Mussoorie must have wandered through its vast spaces. I walk down the rambling corridors, the empty sun-drenched lounge, lost in the memory of happy times, and Nandu catches up with me. Together we walk through the deserted dining room. He jokes: 'This hotel is so big that by the time you get from the reception to the room, we could have charged you for a day!'

Going past the Writers' Bar, a wave of nostalgia washes over me, I tear myself away, rushing down the steps—those familiar twenty steps—one last time. How well I know things will never be the same again. Suddenly, I hear a shuffling behind me. Is it the ghosts of the past come to bid one last goodbye? Or, is it the wind playing in the gables? Who knows? I move on from door to door, from transept to transept, from corridor to lounge, from ballroom to balcony, tracing a century here and a generation there, in pillar and arch, vault and buttress. And, I will probably end where I began: at the rosewood entrance which throws its massive arch into a work-a-day world, and inside, hoards a treasure trove of memories. Brimming over with the sheer loveliness that comes from wood and stone!

And, for over a hundred years, emperor and clown have walked up these very steps, through this very same arch into a magnificent doorway to history! The Savoy still appears at the time of one last farewell like a shimmering mirage in the memories of those who resonated to its poignant beauty years ago.

# Dehra Dun—A Magical Walk Down Memory Lane

Himmat S. Dhillon

Dehra Dun. A place, yes, but so much more than just another place on the map. Dehra—a name that forces one to take a nostalgic walk down memory lane to a glorious land swathed in a golden sepia tinted light. Time was when Dehra Dun was a quaint town popularly associated with grey heads and green hedges. A place that has ancient associations. Certainly, traditional lore has it that in Vedic times, it was the site of the ashram of none other than the great sage and educator, Drona. That Dehra has kept alive this great tradition of scholarship and high quality education even into modern times is testified by the prevalence of well-known, internationally renowned institutions, here such as the Indian Military Academy, the grand architecture of the Forest Research Institute and the Doon School.

A place where the good citizens would ride in *tongas* that went clip-clopping down streets lined with green hedges in which a huge range of chirruping birds abounded. A place where the swiftly flowing East Canal actually served to bring cold water from the hills that would be let into an elaborate system of smaller brick-built water channels that would gush into individual water tanks that served to nourish each private garden. Today, as one drives along the E.C. Road, the abbreviations standing for East Canal, there is absolutely no trace of the water course. The reason is because the powers that be thought it fit to cover up the water course after laying concrete pipes where the canal once flowed unfettered. In effect, turning the canal into an underground sewer!

Time was when it was not unusual for households to have their own stables for horses that served to pull vehicles that are now only to be seen in museums that ranged from sporty gigs to grand carriages, from stately Victorias to swift Phaetons. Every house had servant quarters, some a dairy and many their own piggery as well as poultry. It was a place where High Tea was a custom that was as indispensable as any of the three main meals. And, yes, the bill of fare was as elaborate as the occasion was sacrosanct. Incidentally, it was 'eaten' in the best British traditions with 'Three Tier Charlies' laden with cream puffs, mince cutlets, pies stuffed with all that was nice, rich plum cakes and scrumptious patties. One would be invited to tea and visitors would take especial care as to their dress and deportment.

In Dalanwala, each house was set amidst its own orchard. In fact, till Independence there actually existed a legislation as to the minimum area in acres that was a mandated requirement before permission was granted for a house to be built in the Dalanwala area. This ensured that it was a magical place where you would grow up amidst *litchi*, jack fruit, pomelo and mango trees. A place where children would play in the shelter of giant trees that watched over them. A place where colourful butterflies flitted through the subtle play of light and shadow amidst sprays of wild orchids on the dark trunks of mango trees laden with nectar sweet pendant *Chausa* mangoes.

Dehra Dun. A place synonymous with home. A place where even today, people strive to live after their retirement. A priceless place where, as a result of the spiralling price of real estate, a plot of land is far beyond the reach of most citizens. A place that an astute adman may sell with the slogan 'where the classy, the rich and the famous aspire to retire! A place where one can savour the cold of clear winter nights as well as the warmth of warm, sunny winter days with azure blue skies even while the rest of the northern plains reel under the depressing damp fogs!'.

It is the strategic geographical location of Dehra Dun at the very base of the majestic abode of the eternal snows that ensures it the title of the gateway to the Garhwal Himalayas. A sleepy town nestled between the Ganges and the Yamuna. A sylvan vale protected on one side by the Himalayas and, on the other, by the Shivaliks. The valley of the Doon. The name serves to conjure up misty images that are magical in themselves. Basmati rice... The story goes that the seeds of this fragrant, long-grained rice reached the Doon Valley as a part of the effects of the deposed ruler of Afghanistan who was forced to live out his days in inglorious exile here after being defeated by the British. Alas, today the Doon basmati is a mere memory as most of the traditional basmati growing areas are rapidly getting colonised by rapacious property developers.

There was a time when the valley was renowned for its beauteous tea gardens in which grew a green tea that commanded a tremendous value in the export market. However, the tea gardens were perhaps the first blow to the forests in the valley, as to set up a tea garden one first needed to fell the dense sal forests. Ironically, this very felling of natural forest resulted in a rise in the temperature here which proved detrimental to the tea industry! Alas, today the pressure upon my green valley is the greatest ever. One actually wonders how long it will be before the tea gardens themselves are gobbled up in the name of development! The fact remains that they are still a green lung in this area!

Ironically, it is the very attraction of the Doon Valley that is proving to be its undoing. Almost every day, stately old bungalows are being pulled down to make way for towering apartment blocks to cater to the great demand to live in the environs of the Doon. However, how many care to consider that the entire region is in zone five, as far as seismic activity is concerned, which means that it is eminently avoidable to construct multi-storey buildings here as there is a great risk of damage during an earthquake?

By far, the best thing about Dehra Dun is that one is still close to nature. Time was when all one had to do was to move a few kilometres in any direction from the hustle and bustle of the clock tower to be in the arms of Mother Nature. Sal forests, the ferny banks of swiftly flowing crystal-clear streams, the gold spots of the *Chital*, the Red Jungle Fowl darting across the burnt sienna of the tracks in the forest... Today, though, these are images from the past.

However, in spite of the great changes, hope still exists and something that is good remains. For all those who are fond of the hills and like to walk, the valley is a staging post to mountain heaven. A walk to Everest Estate, better known as the Park

Estate or simply the Park, is one of the best reasons to make a trip to these hills. However, the moment one gets to The Park, one is saddened by the shabby state that this once stately monument has been reduced to and that too, as a result of its so-called restoration.

To get there, all that one has to do is to get to Mussoorie, take the road to the infamous Lambidhar limestone quarries from the invariably clogged library roundabout. It is an interesting walk along a tree-shaded road once one is past the Mussoorie Modern School and then on through Hathipaon, an intriguing name if nothing else. One tale is that it got to be called Hathipaon because of a nearby knoll that is shaped like an elephant's foot. Anyway, this is an ideal place to top up with cold, clean, refreshing, revitalising water that gushes from a natural spring. Of course, one must wait while those who got here first satisfy their thirst—this is one of the cardinal rules of these lovely hills. This is not the place to push and shove and elbow others out of the way—this is a place where one nods companionably, smiles and does things fair and square. This is a place where the density of vehicles, as well as the blaring horns and the loud music that tends to shatter one's sanity decreases in a pleasing manner to miraculously disappear.

Then, it is an enchanting walk through thickets of Himalayan oak till one is on Cloud's End Road. The air here is crisp and cool and rich with a variety of birdsong. Then, one abruptly comes to the Wishing Well, where wishes never come true. Moreover, no one drinks the water as it is believed that the water guarantees bad luck.

But, don't even for a moment despair; a stone's throw away is a tiny shrine where, hold your breath and cross your fingers, they say every wish comes true. Of course, this is too good to be true. One is informed that only those wishes that will ultimately result in the greater good of all parties involved come to fruition. And, don't forget, the other thing is that only if you are really and truly pure in heart, will your wishes come true. So, now that you are privy to the best kept secret of this little town, here's wishing you all the best. And, do be careful of what you wish for—all things being in order—you just may actually get what you wished for. So, all the best—happy wishing!

One has to take the fork to the left. A determined assault will power you up the steep slope and up pop a couple of traditional *pahari* houses with their sloping roofs and the ubiquitous livestock. A welcome contrast to the oh so 'mardern' ugly blocks of cheesy flats and flashy houses that mushroomed in Mussoorie during the building boom that occurred in the Eighties and Nineties. This pastoral scene, set on gentle meadows is framed by viridian deodars. As one takes in the stately cedars and the green, green grass one can't help wondering how long before overpopulation annihilates this rural idyll. Anyway, for now, this is a good location to set up camp. There is a plentiful supply of water nearby, you are near enough to the town to get provisions and medical help and yet far away to enjoy the peace that nature affords.

Everest Hill is a stark contrast to the wooded walk that preceded it. There are no trees, only thorny scrubby bushes. However, one is constantly amazed to find stands of deodars and loads of *mansura* shrubs that invite the tired wanderer to linger beneath their hospitable boughs. Incidentally, it is the superabundance of the *mansura* bush in these hills that gave Mussoorie its name. However, this is not a resultant of Ma Nature being fickle or even capricious—where there is forest cover invariably is a sign of the absence of limestone or at least, it was just not economically viable to exploit it! It is a sadly ignored fact that wherever there is a depletion of forest cover, in fact, earth cover, wherever the bedrock is exposed to the eye that is precisely where the quarrying of limestone has taken place. The evidence will make even the most hardened soul wince. So much for the way God willed it to be.

The villain of the piece seems to be the limestone mining that has wreaked havoc in these parts. According to one knowledgeable source, these parts have the distinction of boasting of the most pure limestone in the entire world. At best a dubious distinction keeping in view the damage caused by the commercial exploitation of this mineral. In fact, one old-timer avers that the British would say Mussoorie *dead is worth a million times more than Mussoorie alive.* So, that is exactly what has happened and the scars and gashes on these once thickly wooded slopes is evidence enough of the avarice of our fellow-human beings. A sparrowhawk wheels about in the sky—I wonder, if it has found anything to eat. I wonder... I find it highly ironic that the great ornithologist Dr Salim Ali intended to lead an expedition in these very parts to try and find the Mountain Quail, a bird long thought to have become extinct.

At the site of the Park exist a few scrawny-looking deodars which seem a far cry from being anywhere near this fabulous tree of the Gods. Still to be seen are the enormous underground chambers used to collect, compress and store snow. An excellent and eco-friendly way to store and harness the bounty of nature and that too, without giving the benefactor undue stress.

As one sneaks a peek through the dirty glass pane, the fungus-covered walls inside are the colour of an exotic French cheese that has rotted. There are still remnants of the builder's aesthetic sense. An exquisite Doric design ornaments the area along the ceiling of the principal room. The room is in the shape of a bullet—a rectangle capped by a hemisphere! Thick wooden beams, undoubtedly local sal that is reputed to be as strong as steel, provide support to the ceiling. There is a fireplace in every room. The shape of the fireplace in this room is noteworthy—this one is flanked by vaulted Grecian columns and crowned with a mantle in an unusual hemispherical shape. There is a verandah shaped like a quarter that opens up into a dramatic vista that showcases the sheer drop on the side facing the valley.

Everest Estate is an important historic landmark of this region. Colonel George Everest, Surveyor General of India, after whom the highest mountain in the world is named, lived in this house from 1833 to 1843. It is one of the great ironies of all time that he was not even aware of the existence, let alone significance of this great massif that by the efforts of mere men, came to bear his name and caused him to become part of the eternal magic of Chomolungma. It was in the role of the superintendent of the Great Trigonometrical Survey that he completed the Great Meridianal Arc of India. He requested permission to move a part of his office to Mussoorie, ostensibly for the purpose of bringing to a satisfactory termination the two northern sections of the Great Arc. An interesting bit of trivia that very often gets missed out is the fact that the Park House was built in the year 1830 by a certain Colonel Whish. Everest purchased the estate from the good colonel in 1833.

Access to the Park was by an unsafe track until the Pioneers cut out a path that in those rough and ready times passed for a good and safe road! However, the government had never been very happy with the office of the Surveyor General of India being situated in Mussoorie. In 1843, Everest received his marching orders and dutifully disposed of Park Estate with a heavy heart. Amongst its illustrious list of subsequent owners have been Col Skinner, John Mackinnon, and Chowdhury Pooran Singh, the legendary criminal lawyer of the Doon Valley.

Sandeep Singh, the son of the late Chowdhury Pooran Singh is a mine of information on the Park. He recalls living in the main house and farming in the estate when it was held by their family. Life in those days was still very much like it was in Everest's time at the Park. During their ownership, the house still retained its original Victorian furniture and ambience.

Everest's observatory-cum-office is still standing at the Park. Local lore has it that this is where he would receive visitors, especially those whom he considered too infra dig to be entertained at his residence, which was a few hundred feet away. However, the one constituent of Park Estate that never fails to excite even the most frigid visitor is its row of 'bibikhanas' that are situated within a yelling distance from the main house. According to knowledgeable locals, these stone walls housed the quarters of a retinue of native mistresses who would help to warm Everest's bed on cold winter nights!

Until a few years ago, the roof was made of sloping tin sheets, which is an essential requirement in these hills. 'When there was not a single leak in Everest's time and we remained dry under that very tin roof, then what was the need to go in for a flat roof?' asks Sandeep Singh when informed about the change.

Today, the visitor would find that the house is topped by a flat, reinforced concrete roof. Anyone who is even remotely familiar with this part of the planet would tell you that this is the most asinine thing to do in this region, where torrential downpours and a few feet of snowfall are but routine facts of life. However, this seems to be the result of some misguided

'renovation' work after the Park was acquired. Today, the most pertinent question that needs to be raised is not how much longer will the legacy of Sir John Everest remain standing, but whether the valley of the Doon will be able to preserve its character in the coming years?

# Travelling with a Phantom

Sumanta Banerjee

It was a sunny December morning. After my usual jogging in Gandhi Maidan, I was resting, watching the children playing cricket. All of a sudden, there appeared this lady— may be in her late thirties, of medium height and solid build with a round face—briskly walking up and down. She was dressed in a full-sleeved white blouse tightly knotted round the neck, and a sari that descended in numerous folds right down to her feet—without even a tiny glimpse of the female midriff that is on display so much in Dehra Dun today! And; her feet; again, were similarly fully cushioned in a pair of tiny brown moccasins, peeping out every now and then like mice from under the massive folds of her sari. After a few rounds of walks, she finally decided to take rest—and slumped down at the end of the bench that I was occupying. She brought out an old paper fan, and began to wave it around her face. And then, she turned towards me and said in a strangely archaic fashion: 'Babu, may I seek your help?' Although a bit surprised by the term of her address, I said: 'Yes, ma'am.' She then came out with her request: 'Please...I'm very tired...Can you please help me to walk down to the gates?'

In a mood of chivalry, I rose and took her by her arms and led her to the gates of Gandhi Maidan. As soon as we came out from the main gates on Rajpur Road, I was struck by a blast of cold wind which blinded my eyes. When I could regain my senses, I found that it had become dark. It was night, with a few lamp-posts around emitting a pale lemon green light. I turned right and couldn't find Astley Hall, but made out the shapes of some shops beyond, dimly lit from inside. In front, there was no Kwality, but a long deserted stretch, with a few houses in the distance, their tiny lights glimmering.

As I stood shivering in the cold, I heard sounds of a slow trot and soon a horse-driven carriage came to a halt in front of me. From its window, there peered out the face of the woman whom I had escorted a few minutes ago from Gandhi Maidan. She no longer looked tired, and appeared to be quite chirpy. But still very formal in her manners, she addressed me in her old fashioned way: 'I am extremely grateful to you, Babu, for helping me. Can I have the pleasure of giving you a lift and dropping you at your residence?'

Since I found no sign of any Bikram or scooter around, I accepted her offer, and stepped into the carriage. Taking a seat opposite her, I apologised: 'Sorry, ma'am, my home is far away—a village called Johrigaon.' At this, she said in a stentorian voice: 'You will be dropped wherever you want to. But before that, I have to attend to some important work—if you don't mind.' I hastily assured her: 'Certainly, ma'am!' By now, she was looking like a formidable schoolmarm, and I was increasingly beset by an uncanny feeling of helplessness in her presence—she having assumed the role of taking me under her protection. It was so different from what it was a few minutes ago!

The carriage trotted along Rajpur Road. It was rather eerie. The houses and shops with which I was familiar seemed to have disappeared behind a grey fog. After a number of twists and turns, the carriage stopped in front of a building—a rather modest looking structure with the words 'Presbyterian Church' inscribed on its arch. My companion stepped out, and then turned to me: 'Babu, we are Christians. If it does not offend your religious feelings, can I invite you to spend a few minutes at our home? My father will be delighted to meet you.' I got down and followed her. She took me behind the main building, and we entered a small cottage. An elderly gentleman came up to greet us. He was clad in *dhoti* and *kurta*, with a Kashmiri shawl leisurely spread across his shoulders. 'Meet my father,' she said, introducing him to me, 'Bhubanmohan Bosu. He is the headmaster of the A.P. Mission Church School of Dehra Dun.' Unable to check my Bengali parochial sentiments, I said to her: 'Arrey, you should have told me that you're from Bengal!' We then slipped into Bengali. Sliding down in his leather-cushioned armchair, Bhubanmohan broke out into loud laughter and said: 'This girl is a madcap! How did you get into her clutches?' The daughter meanwhile, dropping her schoolmarmish manners, wagged a finger at me and said: 'You'll have to wait for me till I come back', and disappeared.

Bhubanmohan kept me engaged in a fascinating conversation—an exchange between my curiosity and his memories. 'We are from a village called Mahanad in Hooghly in West Bengal,' he said. He then began his story: 'This girl, whom you've met, was our first child. She was born on 3 August 1860. We had earlier converted to Christianity, and we baptised her as Chandramukhi. I moved to Dehra Dun as a teacher, and when she was old enough, I admitted her to a girls' school here.' Bhubanmohan, with his eyes sparkling, said: 'Her teachers were so impressed by her performance that Reverend Heron, who was the superintendent of the Dehra Dun Girls' School, made a special appeal to the Calcutta University in 1875, for allowing her to sit for the Entrance school-leaving examination—which till then had remained debarred for girl students.' What happened? To my query, Bhubanmohan said: 'Since the Calcutta University could not depart from its rules, they sent the question papers to her home to test her ability. Her answers, which she did on her own, bowled over the examiners, who recommended that in future, girls along with boys, must be allowed to sit for exams.' With a twinkle in his eyes, Bhubanmoan added: 'Shouldn't you regard my daughter as a pioneer of what you folks describe as the feminist movement?'

Listening to the old man, I kept rummaging my memory. Chandramukhi? The name sounded familiar—yet so distant in time! My memory went haywire. As if guessing my thoughts, Bhubanmohan smiled and asked me: 'Surprised? Aren't you?' Again, with the old sparkle lighting up his eyes, he announced proudly: 'My daughter was the first woman to graduate from Calcutta's Bethune College in 1883 and later to obtain a Master of Arts degree in English literature from the Calcutta University.' But before the old man could proceed further, his daughter came in. She was in her old sartorial attire—the only addition being a thick leather portfolio that she clutched in a tight grasp. She looked a bit older now in the light of the lamps that lit the room. I could discover a few strands of grey hair, and signs of wrinkles underneath her eyes—although as alert as before. She was back in her schoolmarmish role, and immediately started lecturing her father: 'Oh, Baba! Stop your prattle!', and then suddenly lapsed into a childish tone to remind him: 'And Baba, I was not the only girl to become the first woman graduate. Don't you remember Kadambini, my classmate, who also sat with me for the exams that year?' Bhubanmohan nodded his head and said: 'Ah yes! I remember now. Didn't she become a medical doctor?'

At this, I jumped up. Everything now fell in place. Of course, I had read about the duo—Chandramukhi Bose and Kadambini Bose! The pioneering pair of women, who blazed a trail in nineteenth-century Calcutta. Kadambini was the first and only woman who dared to enter the city's medical college, went to England for further education and after completing her studies in Edinburgh and Glasglow, came back to Calcutta to join the Lady Dufferin Hospital as a senior doctor. And, Chandramukhi? I now looked back at her. She was standing there—her stern face now about to break into a shy smile. I was in a daze. In a faltering tone I asked her: 'But...in the past...weren't you also...the first Bengali principal of the Calcutta Bethune College?'

She immediately assumed her imperious tone, and said: 'What do you mean by "in the past"? I am still the principal of the college. I'll retire next year.' Even before I could recover from this shock of the total disarray of time and space, Chandramukhi said in an impatient tone: 'Come along, young man! I'll drop you home.' She then turned to her father and said: 'Baba, don't wait for me for dinner. I'll be late. There's a very important meeting this evening.' I took leave of Bhubanmohan—both of us promising to meet again.

I followed Chandramukhi as she strode to the carriage that was waiting outside. We stepped into it, and the horses began to trot their way through the lanes. Once ensconced within the carriage, I ventured to ask her: 'But tell me ma'am, why have

SAHITYA SAMITY

you come all the way from Calcutta to Dehra Dun?' She retorted: 'Why not? It's my town. This is where I was brought up. And, this is where I met the man I married—Pandit Keshabananda Mamgain.' That put an end to my further queries. Meanwhile, the carriage had reached the main road. But it did not look like the Rajpur Road that I had known. There were no neon-lit shopping plazas or eating joints. As the carriage sped past, I could catch glimpses of a few scattered bungalows lit up by the lanterns of our carriage, followed by unending stretches of huge sal trees disappearing in the darkness of the forest. The carriage finally stopped at the gates of a building. Here, I finally heaved a sigh of relief when I could recognise the Swamy Ramtirth Mission Ashram—a familiar landmark of Dehra Dun which had suddenly cropped up in this bizarre itinerary of mine along a strange city. I got back my bearings. So, when Chandramukhi asked me whether I would like to join her at the 'very important meeting' that she was attending, I readily agreed and got down from the carriage.

But to my dismay, I found that it was not the Ramtirth Mission Ashram that we know today. It was a small cottage of sorts, opening inside into a big hall, filled with a large gathering. At the end of the hall, there was a table with three chairs—the central one vacant, the one on the left occupied by an elderly lady, the other on the right by a bearded gentleman. Chandramukhi walked up and occupied the vacant chair. I managed to locate an empty seat in the middle of the audience, which I found was mainly made up of Bengali babus—with a sprinkling of ladies. While the men, some sporting trimmed beard, were mostly dressed in three-piece suits, the women were attired in the style of Chandramukhi—in saris and full-sleeved blouses.

Meanwhile, Chandramukhi had got down to business. She opened her leather portfolio, brought out a sheaf of papers, and began to address the audience: 'Ladies and gentlemen, we have gathered here today, in this December evening of the year 1900, for an important event—the establishment of a literary society, to be called the Bangla Sahitya Samiti. As you know, wherever Bengalis go, depending on their religious beliefs, they either set up a Kalibari or a masjid or a church, or a Brahmo Samaj temple. But let us strike out on a different course in this beloved town of ours, Dehra Dun. Let us bring together all these expatriate Bengalis here—irrespective of their religious beliefs and creeds—around the common cultural heritage of their language and literature.' Stopping in the midst of her address, she turned towards the elderly lady who was sharing the dais with her, and said: 'Let me introduce to you first Hemanta Kumari Chaudharani, a leading member of the Brahmo Samaj, who is the Director of Education of the Patial Raj Estate.' She then turned to her left and introduced the bearded gentleman sitting there: 'Meet Janab Kafil Ahmed Chaudhary, who is a senior scientific officer in the Forest Research Institute in Dehra Dun.' Both of them rose, folded their palms in *namashkar*, and the audience clapped their hands. Chandramukhi then, resuming her address, said: 'We are fortunate in having these two illustrious personalities among us today on this solemn occasion. May I request them now to inaugurate our library which will be open to all of you henceforth?'

Hemanta Kumari and Kafil Ahmed walked up to a huge wooden cupboard in a corner of the hall, and each held out its glass doors from either side—displaying rows of books, neatly stacked in the shelves. Soon after this official inauguration, the audience broke up into a chattering crowd, every one moving up to the cupboard to select his or her favourite book. As soon as I could trace Chandramukhi, I dragged her into a corner and said in a hushed tone: 'But, ma'am, you may not know—the Bangla Sahitya Samiti and the library are no longer here. They have shifted to Karanpur.' At this, Chandramukhi looked excited, and taking my arms said: 'Can you take me there now?'

We came out and got into her carriage. I instructed the driver to go straight along Rajpur Road and then turn right to E.C. Road. By the time we reached there, the skies seemed to have cleared and I could recognise the surroundings. As we entered a lane, I pointed out with a sense of pride the signboard to Chandramukhi: 'Look, this street carries the name Bengali Library Road. It leads to our Bangla Sahitya Samiti.' She was all smiles. And then, when we reached the Samiti building, she was overwhelmed by the sight of the gate with its arch carrying the name of the society that she had found along with her friends. We went up to the library. I introduced Chandramukhi to Biplab, who is the present secretary of our Samiti, and who also functions as the librarian. He took out a steel chair, dusted it and offered it to her.

Chandramukhi looked around the library. Although every corner of the room was filled with steel almirahs packed with books, there was no human soul around—barring the three of us. It was a far cry from the crowded scene that we had witnessed a few moments ago. She kept shifting her glance to the bulk of books tied up in ropes, which remained heaped upon the top of the almirahs—untouched and unread. Guessing her thoughts, Biplab said apologetically: 'Didi, we don't have the resources to expand our library to accommodate all those books.' Chandramukhi flared up: 'But where are your members? Can't they spare money to build another room? Don't they want to read those books?' At this, Biplab, with a sad smile on his face, said: 'There are no readers of serious stuff here today, Didi!'

Chandramukhi seemed to shrivel up. She crouched down in the chair, and after a moment, held out her hands, looked at us and asked in a shaky voice: 'Can you take me back?' Fearing that she might be feeling sick, I said: 'Certainly, I'll take you home.' She raised her hands and said: 'No! No! Not home. There'll be no one there now.' She then looked around uncertainly, and asked: 'There was a...a cemetery in Dehra Dun...is it still there?'

As I stood flummoxed by this strange question, Biplab came to my help. He held Chandramukhi by her hands, raised her from the chair and said: 'I know, Didi, where you want to go. Let me take you there.' As he gently led her out, I heard him saying: 'But Didi, that graveyard has been taken over...long since...the tombstone is no longer there...no one knows where you were buried.'

# IMA, FRI, The Doon School and RIMC

Kunal Verma

*Where the mind is without fear and the head is held high*

— Rabindranath Tagore

Born in Dehra Dun, I honestly used to think I'd never get out of the place. Till I was sixteen, I rarely did! Both my grandparents had, post-retirement, opted to settle down in the quiet environs of the Doon Valley, and as a result, my childhood was a whirl between the Army Cantonment (where we lived in just about every possible locality), Dallanwala, where my mother's side had settled and Clement Town, where my father's parents had this huge bungalow with a multitude of fruit trees. To claim that I knew each and every nook and cranny of the valley wouldn't be an idle boast, for the surrounding regions were also as much one's playground as the main city itself.

In the early 1960s, Dehra Dun was quite the one-horse town where the preferred mode of transport was the 'tonga'—a horse-drawn carriage that clip-clopped its way through *ghanta ghar* and to other exotic locations, the equine every now and then raising its tail and adding to the goodly smells that wafted through the air. My earliest visual memories are of various types of horse-drawn buggies, both the civilian and the military types, for my father was then a Captain posted at the Indian Military Academy as a Platoon Commander. Just as the main city was a congested mess of tongas, cycles, cars and handcarts, IMA was at the opposite end of the spectrum. Few places in the country can match the splendour of the Academy, which when combined with the equally imposing and contiguous Forest Research Institute (FRI), can easily boast of being the architectural and esthetic showpiece of the country.

Two decades after having 'escaped' from the clutches of the Doon Valley, I was offered the rare honour of shooting the IMA film, *The Making of a Warrior*. Delighted at the prospect of producing a film in my 'home town', I was soon submerged in research material as I flipped through the pages of history.

Towards the end of the 1920s, the political leadership of the Indian National Congress began to press for the recruitment of Indian officers into the British Indian Army. In the face of this growing demand, the Montague–Chelmsford Reforms enabled the first few batches of Indian 'Gentleman Cadets' to be sent to Sandhurst for training. Subsequently, at the Round Table Conference in London in 1930, it was recommended that India should have its very own military academy. Accordingly, a

committee under the chairmanship of Field Marshal Sir Philip Chetwode, the then Commander-in-Chief of the British Indian Army, recommended that the erstwhile Railway College in Dehra Dun, that had the appropriate buildings and the requisite land, should be acquired for the purpose.

On 1 October 1932, the Military Academy, then commanded by Brigadier LP Collins, DSO, OBE, became functional with a course strength of forty Gentleman Cadets; the course, which nicknamed itself the 'Pioneers', had fifteen direct entries, a similar number selected from the ranks through the Kitchner College, Nowgaon, while the remaining ten were selected from the various existing Princely States. The Gentlemen Cadets were simply known as '*Gee Cee log*' in Hindi, and GCs in English!

The formal inauguration of the Academy took place in December 1932, when Field Marshal Chetwode made his historic speech from which is extracted the stirring lines that were to become the Credo of the Academy: '*The safety, honour and welfare of your country come first, always and every time. The honour, welfare and comfort of the men you command come next. Your own ease, comfort and safety come last, always and every time.*'

In 1934, before the first course had passed out, Lord Willingdon, the Viceroy of India, presented the Academy Colours on behalf of the King of Britain. The parade was commanded by Under-Officer GC Smith Dun, who was an ethnic Burmese Karen. Subsequently, when the Pioneers passed out of the Academy, Dun, who was extremely short in stature and after the Second World War was nicknamed by Field Marshal Slim as the 'Four Foot Colonel', also won the prestigious Sword of Honour and later, rose to the rank of General when he was appointed Chief of Army Staff in the Burmese Army. Two other

GCs also went on to command their respective armies—Sam Manekshaw (later Field Marshal and the Chief of Army Staff of the Indian Army during the Bangladesh War of 1971) and Musa Khan Hazara (later, General and the Commander of the Pakistan Army during the Indo–Pak War of 1965). K. Bhagwati Singh (later, Major-General and the father of the former Naval Chief, Admiral Madhvendra Singh) had the distinction of holding the first ever Indian Commission—known universally as 'IC'—number one!

Between December 1934 and May 1941, sixteen regular courses had passed out and only 524 Gentlemen Cadets were commissioned. World War II changed the pace of life at the Academy drastically, with 3,887 cadets passing out of the Academy between August 1941 and January 1946. In order for the Academy to grow, additional land was brought into use and a large number of temporary structures were built, some of which continue to be used even to this day. The two earliest residential blocks were named after the first two Commandants, Brigadiers Collins and Kingsley.

After Independence, Brigadier Thakur Mahadeo Singh, DSO, became the first Indian Commandant of the Academy. Like the rest of the Army, the partition of the country resulted in the movable property of the Academy being divided between India and Pakistan. Two months after freedom dawned on the subcontinent, the Gentlemen Cadets opting for Pakistan left the Academy for their new home.

Today, the Academy has four battalions—Cariappa, Thimayya, Manekshaw and Bhagat, each with three companies that together house 1,600 GCs. Originally, when it was acquired from the Railway College, the total area of the Academy was just over 200 acres, which has now expanded to seven times that size. The lush green environs of the Academy, with its mix of colonial and modern architecture set amidst a variety of gigantic trees , provides the ideal atmosphere for the training of generation after generation of Gentlemen Cadets.

Linking the Indian Military Academy to the Forest Research Institute is the stunningly picturesque FRIMA golf course, where during a game you can often see wild jungle fowl hurtle across the narrow tree-lined fairways. For all practical purposes, the two contiguous institutions are difficult to tell apart, especially when the GCs are out on a cross-country run. Established in 1906, FRI predates the IMA by more than two and a half decades and it is synonymous with the development of scientific forestry in the subcontinent. Eardley-Wilmot, who was the Inspector-General of Forests at the turn of the century, must get most of the credit for having conceived and started the initial work to set up the Forest Research Institute. With the foothills of the Himalayas as a backdrop, the 450 hectares is dominated by the main building that marries the Greco–Roman and Colonial styles of architecture. This massive architectural edifice, with a plinth area that exceeds 5,800 square metres, houses offices, classrooms, equipped laboratories, library, herbarium, arboreta, printing press and experimental field areas for conducting forestry research, quite in keeping with the best of its kind anywhere in the world. Its six museums that are spread over 2,400 square metres are a valuable source of scientific information. Designed by C.G. Blomfield and built by Sardar Ranjit Singh, the building was inaugurated in 1929.

Forestry in the subcontinent can be divided into two parts—the pre and post-FRI periods. From the early days of the nineteenth century, the British Government was extremely sensitive about the supply of teak for the Royal Navy, which at that time was mainly restricted to the Malabar Coast. In northern India, sal forests were being very heavily cut for home consumption. The felling carnage was quite uncontrolled and as per records, the forests were in a terrible condition. In other parts of the country, the situation was as bad—the Punjab was suffering from the exploitation of deodar in particular, and the fuel shortage in the hill areas was extremely acute. Quite contrary to the generally held view that at that time India was teeming with jungles and wildlife, the situation was in real terms quite grim even then.

After the turmoil surrounding the First War of Independence in 1857, the British turned their attention towards land management and forestry in a big way. India was one of the first countries in the world that was to have a stated scientific management of its forests, and in 1864, the Imperial Forest Department was started with Dr Dietrich Brandis, a German botanist, appointed as the Inspector-General of Forests. The Department owed its origin also to the growing needs of the railways for timber and firewood, and three years later, the Imperial Forest Service came into being. One of the reasons for homing onto the Doon Valley as its headquarters may well have been the availability of the sal tree, which was ideal for railway sleepers.

The officers appointed to the Service between 1867 and 1905 were trained initially in France and Germany, then in the later years, almost exclusively in England. This practice was to continue despite the Imperial Forest College being established in the neighbouring Chandbagh estate in 1914. Only in 1926 did the onus of training foresters shift in its entirety to FRI. Since its inception, each of the Institutes branches—silviculture, botany, entomology, chemistry and utilisation added tremendously to the knowledge and development of Indian forests. During the Second World War, the utilisation section in particular, played a key role when the use of secondary timber and economy in the employment of wood and other forest produce became a vital necessity.

FRI's history apart, the 1,000-acre campus is even today a virtual environmental delight—the perfect example of the wild, green earth! As a child, I have vivid memories of a large enclosure that housed a number of spotted deer, or *chital* as they are more commonly known. Over the years, some 2,000 sample plots under exotic species like eucalyptus, poplars, tropical pines, acacias, bamboo and a host of others have provided data for compiling yield and volume tables for over 120 tree species while other studies have helped gain a better understanding of forest ecology. In 1991, FRI was given the status of a Deemed University by the Government of India.

As Dehra Dun started to emerge as the home of major Institutions in the country, the game of musical chairs continued; the Imperial Forest College moved to FRI in 1935 and Chandbagh, along with additional grounds acquired from the descendants of Colonel Skinner's estate, was handed over to the Indian Public Schools Society to set up the Doon School within the 69-acre environs. Sometimes called 'the Eton of India', Doon School has developed its own characteristic style and ethos over the years.

Satish Ranjan Das, the founder of the Doon School, was one of pre-Independence India's eminent barristers and a member of the Executive Council of the Viceroy. His mission was to constitute India's first public school in an era when 'Chief's Colleges' were the ultimate school experience. The Doon School was meant to provide the youth of the country with an opportunity to get an all-round education, based on an adaptation of the English public school system on India's tradition-enriched soil. Like the

IMA, the creation of The Doon School was mainly due to the zeal of a group of nationalists in the pre-Independence period, primarily to produce a new generation of leaders who could guide the nation after Independence.

The school's first Headmaster was a science teacher from Eton, Arthur E. Foot, who had never visited India until then. One of his first actions after accepting the position offered to him was to recruit J.A.K. Martyn from Harrow as his deputy. From its very inception, The Doon School set itself the highest possible standards, which aimed at getting recognised among the ten best schools in the world. In a letter to a parent, another master from that era, Jack Gibson (who subsequently was the principal of the National Defence Academy and Mayo College) encapsulated the school's mission when he wrote: '...each boy... must train himself to think clearly so that he will be willing to come to conclusions that may be different from what he has expected and may point to something different from what we were brought up to believe to be the accepted order. He must train his body to undergo hardships and be prepared for unexpected discomforts, and above all, he must awaken and sharpen his sympathies for and understanding of people outside his own class and circle.'

Amidst the sylvan surroundings of The Doon School, five hundred-odd Doscos are divided into different houses—Hyderabad, Jaipur, Kashmir, Tata and the latter-day addition, Oberoi House. For most of us who had the privilege of studying there, The Doon School years are even more memorable because of the time spent on mid-term breaks and weekends in the foothills of the Himalayas, or in exploring the river valleys of two of the greatest rivers that hem the Doon Valley from two flanks—the Ganga and the Jamuna.

Over the years, the Doon School has produced a Prime Minister, various Chief Ministers and other notable personalities across a diverse variety of professions.

The Doon Valley is today dotted with schools and educational institutions, each with a fairly impressive history of its own. Among them, RIMC (Rashtriya Indian Military College) is perhaps, one of the oldest. Established in 1922 as the Prince of Wales Royal Military College, it was to be the nursery for Indian cadets who were to be sent to Sandhurst for further training. Spread across 134 acres of lush green countryside, it is not far from their arch rivals, The Doon School, against whom generations of Rimcollians have earned their spurs on the playing fields of the two institutions.

While at the RIMC, the boys are known as cadets and the institution grooms them right from the start to don the mantle of India's future military leaders. Most Rimcollians make their way to the National Defence Academy in Khadakwasala en route to the IMA / Air Force Academy / Naval Academy, from where they get commissioned into the Services. General K.S. Thimayya, one of India's most dedicated and respected soldiers, was the first to achieve a four star ranking; counting the Pakistan Armed Forces, seven other Rimcollians have so far had the distinction of becoming Chiefs of their respective Arms. Lt General P.S. Bhagat won the Victoria Cross while Major Som Nath Sharma was the first Indian to get the coveted Param Vir Chakra in November 1947 in Kashmir.

Among the laws that govern human behaviour, institutions are identified with a social purpose that transcends the individual, often forming the bedrock on which national dreams are built. It is unlikely that any other city or region in the country would have had such a far-reaching impact on the rest of the nation and even our immediate surrounding countries. FRI, RIMC, IMA and The Doon School have each played a major role in the development of free India, as have the many other institutions based in Doon. The little Valley that nestles in the lap of the Himalayas and the Shivalik mountains can certainly hold its head extremely high!

# A Journey into a New Life

Florence Pandhi

October 29th 1968. London–Delhi–Mussoorie. The most exciting journey of my life. A journey that brought me five thousand miles from the regularity of the West, with all its creature comfort, paid annual holidays, utopian social security, predictable life-style, insular habits, and an ambient temperature just above freezing. A journey whose last lap on *terra firma* began at what appeared to be a broken down, bombed-out airport called Palam at Delhi. The discomfort was enormous. English winter clothes of wool, nylon and leather are not *de rigeur* apparel in temperatures soaring into the nineties. I made my way down the gangway of the plane onto the tarmac airstrip. It was a Turkish bath, enveloping me in steam. In the dark, I struggled over mounds of gravel and grey sand with the signs of newly constructed buildings looming ahead. My hand baggage weighed a tonne. I felt ridiculously incongruous in my attire as

I entered the arrival lounge. Construction material lay everywhere, as passengers stumbled towards a makeshift customs counter.

Bedlam prevailed. Separated by a rope, hordes of clamouring, wildly gesticulating, anxious, deliriously happy and indescribably noisy people made their presence known. They clung to improvised barriers, trying to squeeze themselves through the customs-check point. Then, by sheer force of numbers, they poured through to mingle with delighted passengers. Such determination! There was an avalanche of joyous relatives, tears, hugs, shaky limbs ably assisted by young bucks, howling babies, children dancing around, and all of it resounding with a babble of incomprehensible tongues.

Pandemonium reigned and no one cared. Customs officers blithely ignored the flood of intruders. Quickly, I was surrounded by a group of Indians who had more of an idea who I was, rather than the other way around. An old man leaning on his stick, middle-aged ladies with their heads covered, and shy, fragile little girls with enormous eyes pressed against me, embracing me and smiling in welcome. Helpless and bewildered, I found myself being swept along with the noise and heat, having lost my independence, towards my new life.

We seemed to be enveloped in a murky darkness. Outside of the airport, the road lamps gave a weary pale yellow light. A couple of large, ugly cars, later to be known as Ambassadors, were to be our chariots to the Maidens Hotel in the centre of Delhi. Each car was packed beyond belief, as relatives piled in on top of each other. Whoever was destined to be the driver, could not possibly attempt to use the rear view mirror, as his vision was blocked with heads and torsos of a gabbling mass. Slowly, we inched forward into a lawless terrain. Vehicles of every description crowded around us, each one desperate to fill up the space in front of our car bonnet. The head-lamps of the car blinked weakly like candle light in a breeze, sensing the direction rather than illuminating the road.

Out of nowhere, we found ourselves in the midst of a brilliantly lit, hued like a rainbow, straggling, dancing, utterly deafening procession of people, blocking the road in gay abandon. The trombonists vied with the trumpets, the drummers with the singer, all bent on creating total anarchy, as they wended their way along the road. A magnificently caparisoned horse carried two spangled and garlanded figures. Unable to inch forward, it stood statue-like, whilst the gargantuan brass band screeched its cacophony into the night sky. The sound thundered and heaved, as male dancers of all ages whirled around with bundles of currency notes held high. I hugged my ears to protect them against this auditory exhibitionism. What, in heaven's name was I witnessing? A wedding party. A far cry from the traditionally nervous English groom, twisting his fingers, hunting for the ring, and clammily praying in the church vestibule, that his tardy bride-to-be would not at the very last minute, jilt him at the altar!

That first night at the Maidens Hotel was one of splendid insomnia. The British Raj in India came alive as if I was reading the books I had devoured in England in preparation for this journey. Could there have been a bigger bathroom anywhere? Its preserved antiquity displayed a tub resting on the paws of a lion, and an incredible piece of Victoriana—a porcelain basin decorated with tiny pink roses, with its matching pitcher. Their surface had millions of miniscule crackles in the glaze that spoke of age. Large brass faucets adorned the tub, allowing warm water to languidly pour into its deep interior.

The adjoining suite had a ceiling that vaulted into infinity. I could humbly visualise a modern English double-storeyed, suburban, semi-detached house being placed, without difficulty, into my cathedral-sized bedroom. From somewhere in the shadowy heights, a long pole descended to suspend, in animation, a ponderously revolving two-bladed fan. Its black arms rotated with dignity, creaking at each revolution, graciously wafting currents of hot, stale air throughout the night. I lay on a giant bed, feeling with each passing hour like the princess and the pea. The mattress resisted me and refused to yield to my need for sleep.

My two non-English speaking companions, my future mother-in-law and her eldest daughter-in-law, tried incomprehensibly to include me in their desultory conversation. They, and the fan droned on through the long hours, joined periodically by a *crrr crrr crrr*, belonging to a strange new insect world. They felt no need to let the night melt into darkness, so the wan yellow wall lights glowed until dawn took over the sky.

The day came alive in a spectacular crackle of activity. I was now part of a family, who began the daily grind with the noise of ringing telephones, visitors calling, appointments before and after breakfast, endless trays of tea, frantic schedules, plenty of humour, and the ear-shattering volume of conversational Punjabi. Papaji, my eldest brother-in-law to-be, was in volcanic form, setting the pace for us all to follow in the next twenty-four hours.

Anglo-Indian breakfasts in colonial hotels are strange and wondrous. Is this the cuisine that our British Tommies used to crave for? Limp cornflake curls lying in thin, sweet, warm milk; tea served with liberal quantities of hot milk, draped with a congealed skin of protein; and the *piece de resistance*—cold potato cutlets served with a lurid, sweet, blood red concoction of tomato sauce. By afternoon, gustatory immoderation had seared that memory from my mind. I had been transported to

Delhi's ancient walled city and found myself weeping tears of wonder over the victual excesses of sambhar and dosa from a South Indian street-stall. My fair hair and complexion, plus the incongruous sari draped around me, drew enormous attention from street urchins and passers-by. I was the only European to be seen, and to be the cynosure of all eyes was discomforting.

The exodus to Dehra Dun was about to commence. The promised early morning start had receded to late afternoon. The family hung around waiting with patience for the patriarch to announce the moment of departure. I felt strangely disjointed from lack of sleep, kaleidoscopic visuals, and the physical exhaustion of tearing around Delhi behind hyperkinetic relatives. Time had become elastic in the confusion and haste of the day. Punctuality has never been a strong point of mine; but I was to rapidly discover a way of life that demanded schedules and at the same time, ridiculed them with consummate ease.

In the dwindling hours of light, our party of nine crushed into one car, streaked through a dream sequence of travelogue village scenes. Weary oxen winding their way home; camels languidly swaying with their heads held high; octroi posts; and overcrowded cartloads of dusty villagers. I crushed myself against the open car window, choking with exhaust fumes and dust, and all the while, fascinated and hypnotised by the unfolding panorama. Frequently, we stopped the car to allow its occupants to stretch squashed limbs, search for toilet facilities for the women, and partake of refreshments from wayside shops. As dusk fell, the air was heavy with wood smoke, and the only sign of habitation was the occasional glimpse of an oil lamp glowing in a hut near the road.

The highway was frightening, dark and endless. Roaring monsters spewing fumes charged us time and time again. They flashed their headlights in anarchic Morse patterns, alternating beams of brilliant blinding madness with sharp staccatos of pitch darkness. Still, we raced on. Sometimes, high on the crown of the road, and when faced with the colossal onslaught of a death defying diesel mountain, we rushed silently to safety through thick clouds of yellow dust that idled at the sides of the road.

The towns that we passed through wore a deserted, fortified appearance. There were no elegant, well-designed shop windows being viewed at leisure by sauntering promenaders. I only saw wooden boards and rolling shutters, no pavements, and the occasional vague yellow light hanging aimlessly from an isolated concrete pole—the impression was one of barricades and fear. I recalled warehouses in England in neglected parts of cities; the similarity and shabbiness was there. I could not see the swank of commercialism and the brassy lure of neon signs.

A shadowy stop in a gloomy deserted place—retrospect labelled it as Muzzafarnagar—provided us with bottles of ice cold, almond-flavoured milk, that eased our dust filled, parched throats. We continued to rush endlessly into a surrealistic world of darkness, punctuated by noisy, blinding apparitions that bore down on us. Suddenly, the car would lurch in a desperate attempt to avoid a bullock-cart that instantly appeared from nowhere, or had we appeared from nowhere? With the pallid yellow lights of the car, our visibility was confined to a few feet.

There was a shivering realisation that the air was getting cooler. The car began to climb and twist. The lights dipped and flashed, catching boulders, broken trees, and narrow bends. The gears shifted down as we climbed higher, passing through an eerie, unlit tunnel cut into a rock face. We began to zoom down the highway with no impediment. We were entering Dehra Dun;

a town that seemed to be as deserted as the ones we had left behind.

I climbed the stairs of the flat somnambulantly. I had never felt so tired in my life, physically and mentally. Who cared where we were—Dehra Dun, Timbuktu, or Alaska? Sleep had become an obsession after two nights without it. A weird night was to follow. The bedroom remained lit, like a football stadium. I wondered about Indian habits. Is it a bad thing to sleep without lights? I feared I would be offending my hosts to mention it, as I lay in wakefulness, my eyes glued to the ceiling. It was a night when the electricity beamed in full glory, and the air was rent with screams at regular intervals! Ghastly screams, the clatter of wooden sticks, followed by more screams. Imagination can be a fearful thing, as I let it wonder. Someone surely had died that night.

Sleepless, but keen as mustard, I rose to face a new day. Enquiries as to who had been done to death brought bemused stares. The night watchman had to keep himself awake, and more importantly, he had to wake the household periodically to ensure his job permanency. No noise, no pay.

My first day in Dehra Dun was crisp and cool, with a sun peeping through roadside trees that lined the main road of the town. Cyclists zig-zagged around the car, vying with horse drawn carts—Tongas—that carried people who seemed to have all the time in the world to get where they were going. The odd car passed by, and the pace of life was leisurely. Passers-by were dressed in their night suits, some cleaning their teeth by the roadside or reading the newspaper. Others sauntered by with aluminium cans filled with fresh milk.

I looked to my right to see a mountain shrouded at its base with mist. To my left, fresh life was emerging, as shopkeepers swept away the dust of the previous day, chatting amiably with their neighbours, unhurried and relaxed. Crisp air, warm sunshine, and cheerful noisy people. Inquisitiveness, kindness, concern and pleasure met me at every turn. Everyone exuded hospitality and interest. That was Dehra Dun at the end of October 1968.

The next lap of our journey appeared treacherous. The dark, intimidating, snaking route to Mussoorie, forced our car through terrain, only meant for an experienced rally driver. My heart dropped in painful jerks, as hairpin bend followed hairpin bend. I watched with backward glances, as Dehra Dun sank gradually below our vision. Its lights winked and blinked, randomly scattered like jewels on black velvet. We flashed past warning signs that insinuated death for all foolish drivers. Gradients increased and the cold bit in alarmingly. My father-in-law to-be exhorted his grandson to drive with more care. He was a man of few words, great caution, and immensely God-fearing. The almighty had brought his precious son back to the land of his birth, and into the love and care of his family. There should not be the slightest mishap on the ultimate stage of the journey.

The last agonising bend came. The car strained and swung wide. I caught a glimpse of illumination thousands of feet below as the car gasped up the Masonic Lodge stretch to reach the final goal. I stepped out into a bitterly cold night, my breath hanging in droplets. Heavens, I had left this behind in England, but I was better-clad for the weather then! My bare feet were pushed into the flimsiest of sandals, my coat had been stowed into the boot of the car, and my teeth chattered uncontrollably.

I had travelled within three days from the dank, bone-eroding chill of London, through the moist, hot blanket of Delhi, felt the relief of autumn moderation in Dehra Dun, only to sojourn in the freezing winds of an Indian hill station! I was bewildered, overwhelmed, even startled by the turn of events. Nothing I had been told had prepared me for this.

Nestling in the valley down below lay Dehra Dun, in all its black and glittering magnificence. This was my first glimpse of the Doon Valley. Unbeknown to me at that time, this valley would take up more than twenty-five years of my life, and continues to do so, in an attempt that frequently seems futile, to save the relentless encroachment on its green belt and the depredations faced by Rajaji National Park. Encroachments, poachers, building mafia, illegal tree cutting, over-building, and sundry other modern day problems are eroding the rich environmental wealth that has been gifted to its inhabitants. A battle is on for this valley that grows more urgent by the day.

But this was the end of October 1968. I had been given a new life in an entirely extraordinary environment. The future was full of optimism and excitement. I peered down on my future home. From my perch in the mountains, it looked like a good choice.

Life and times of the Savoy.

# Random Thoughts

Karan Thapar

*A reverie at a book-reading*

Sometimes, when you meet a person you can end up seeing them not as they are, but through the prism of memories. In such instances, the past overwhelms the present. It's a strange but wonderful experience. Time somersaults backwards, reality converges with history, and myth and legend with truth.

As I watched Vikram Seth read extracts of his new novel, I found myself transported thirty-two years back in time. We were both at the Doon School. Vikram was in A-form and in his penultimate year. I was in D-form and it was my second term. We were preparing for the school debating competition. Vikram was Debating Captain at Jaipur House. I was the youngest, most inexperienced, member of his team.

'Can't you speak with authority, but without shouting?'

Vikram was sitting cross-legged on his chair. He resembled a petite Buddha with sculpted feet and a small round head. His hair kept falling across his forehead. As a result, even when he sounded angry he never looked it.

I wasn't sure what he meant. At eleven, the difference between authority and a loud voice is not obvious. I cleared my throat, stood up straight and started again.

Vikram closed his eyes. He often does, when he is concentrating. But to speak to a man sitting cross-legged on a chair with his eyes shut can be disconcerting. Try hard as I did to control my voice it started to wander.

'You're singing or at least you're sounding very sing-song,' Vikram's eyes were now open and staring ferociously. 'Remember, you won't win any extra points by trying to seduce the judges with your voice. Speak normally, clearly, fluently and you'll carry conviction.'

Neither then nor now, do I know what he meant. 'Speak like you normally do' is an injunction that baffles me. If I don't speak like myself, whom do I speak like? Yet, when I woke from my reverie it was to find, three decades later, that Vikram was doing exactly that. Of course, he wasn't cross-legged. But the small round head, now slightly balding, was talking clearly, fluently, and the audience was transfixed with conviction.

'What an amazing speaker', whispered Shobha Deepak Singh in my ear. She was sitting beside me on the second row of the Habitat Centre auditorium. Aveek Sircar, Vikram's publisher, was beside her. Earlier, with his help, Shobha had got Vikram to autograph her copy of his book.

'He's just being himself,' Aveek added by way of explanation.

I turned to watch Vikram on the stage but before long, my mind started wandering again and I soon found myself tumbling back into the past. This time, we were in the Rose Bowl, rehearsing for the School's annual play. It was Rattigan's *Winslow Boy.* I was the brutish lawyer. Vikram was directing. The year was 1971. It was his year off between A levels and Oxbridge. It was my last year in School.

Vikram had just explained how he wanted a particular scene done. It was partly description and partly enactment. Despite his lack of height, he's a talented actor. Then, with short quick steps and his head inclined downwards, he walked towards the audience stands to sit down and watch. He crossed his legs, cupped his chin in the palm of one hand and rested his elbow on his raised knee. His other hand held on to his foot.

'Right. Let's see how you do it.'

I started. It was the scene where the lawyer cross-examines the young boy. Vikram wanted me to pretend to be angry. Yet, the anger also had to sound genuine, otherwise the cross-examination would not work. Only after it was over would the truth emerge.

'Not bad. Not bad at all,' Vikram pronounced. He was not given to praise easily and I swelled with pride.

Later, rehearsal over, as we walked back, the April night alight with stars but the air hot and heavy, he came back to the subject.

'The funny thing about anger is that it's not the shouting that communicates it. It comes from deeper inside. It's like love and hate. You have to feel it to sense it.' And then, after a pause he added, 'I suppose, all emotions are the same.'

I returned to the present to find Vikram reading a delicately written extract from his book. Helen is tipsy but excited. Her words are tumbling out. Michael, though detached, is not indifferent. His wit is a foil to her emotion. Their feelings emerge, they grow, they suffuse the context but rarely are they stated.

I have to read this book, I said to myself. I bought it a couple of weeks ago. I like to buy new ones as soon as they are out. It's a sort of one-upmanship I play with myself. But I can be very lazy about reading them. And, Salman Rushdie's new novel put me off Indian authors.

A week later, I've finished the book but the story, its characters and their world is still with me. Like memories of the Doon School, it will merge into a consciousness that will always be there. Vikram, the stories about him, and now his book, will fuse into one. I would not want it otherwise.

If you haven't, I recommend you read *An Equal Music.*

## *The man I call Guru and the debt I owe him*

Time can play tricks with you but there is none more disconcerting than realising that growing old is not the same as growing up. I realised that when I met, after a decade or more, one of the heroes of my childhood. I know him as Guru and although he is definitely that for me, his name is in fact, Gurdial Singh. He was my housemaster at Jaipur House in Doon School. If there is anything in me I could be proud of, he spotted it first, nurtured it and last week, when I had myself forgotten, he reminded me of those qualities. Sadly, by then I had shown how much I had changed.

Guru was in Delhi for the weekend and staying with his nephew Mantaj. I was a guest for dinner. He's seventy-seven, it's more than twenty-seven years since I left school and he must have taught several thousand young boys. Yet, he remembered the littlest things, not just about me but others I had myself forgotten.

At school, Guru was a disciplinarian but also the most liberal human being, who has ever taken to teaching. If that sounds contradictory, well, Guru would say, contradictions are what we are all about. Even today, he wakes up at 4.00 a.m. and is out walking before the sun has risen. He loves Beethoven, mountaineering, geography and Old Doscos.

Guru is the stuff legends are made of, and after twenty-seven years, he has become a legend for me. Last week I realised that legends are also very human. Perhaps, that's why they are legends.

'I gather the School is full of boys who have taken to drink and drugs,' I said, as we sat around the table eating. 'I'm told it's no longer the same.'

Mantaj chimed-in with his agreement. We're the same age. Three decades ago, Guru had taught us, seen us falter, make mistakes and without fuss, put us right. He knows us better than either would care to admit.

'Not really, Karan,' Guru replied after a bit. He was chewing his food carefully and Guru always gives the impression of thirty-two chews for every bite. 'There have always been boys at School who drink, or take drugs. It was the same when you were there, and it won't be any different twenty-five years later. The point is fifteen-year-olds want to experiment and so what if they do? Everyone is entitled to one mistake. The important, thing is to learn from it, not repeat it.'

It took me a while to realise what I was hearing. I was so comfortable in my forty-three-year-old intolerance that I had assumed a false moral correctness for my views. Guru, with his casual, but thoughtful response, shattered that. Kids will be kids and they have a right to err. Except he had not expressed himself so pompously, or so patronisingly.

'Don't be too disturbed by all you hear,' Guru continued. 'Generation after generation, this sort of thing stays the same.'

His words brought back memories of all the things I too had done wrong. The little punishments that had once hurt, but today, are simply anecdotes. They had become the source of the exaggerated after-dinner stories I love to tell, but the lessons behind them I no longer remembered. Guru had just reminded me of the truths I had forgotten.

As I drove home that evening, I realised that in the three decades since Guru had last taught me, I might have grown older but had not necessarily grown up as much. Yet, in the three hours I spent in his company, I caught up with a lot of wisdom I had foolishly forgotten.

## *Founder's Day at Doon*

I've just returned from spending Founder's Day at the Doon School. It was my first, after nearly twenty-eight years. That's such a long time, you actually don't remember what it used to be like. Instead, nostalgia and your own distorted memory have created an impression that takes precedence over reality. But once back, the old truths fall into place.

This year the chief guest was Arun Shourie and in his speech, he complimented the School on its excellence. Arun was generous with his praise and deservedly so. As he spoke, my mind flashed back to the Founder's Day of 1968 (or, may be it was 1969). Morarji Desai was the chief guest. He was also Indira Gandhi's deputy prime minister. Christopher Miller, the last Englishman to serve as headmaster, had invited him and the School was looking its best.

Desai arrived by helicopter, touching down on the sacrosanct main field. He raced through the many and interesting school exhibitions laid on for him. I was twelve and waiting to show him what I could do with pippettes in chemistry. But he was not interested. The photographs of the occasion show him looking over my tiny shoulders towards the exit.

It was Desai's speech that angered and hurt the School. To begin with, he spoke in Hindi, a calculated affront to our English Headmaster, and a language he fully knew the boys could not easily follow. But Desai hated public schools and wanted to rub it in.

What I remember of his speech was, the way he chided the boys for greeting him with a handshake. Why had we not done *namaste,* instead? This, he admonished, was aping the West and forgetting our own culture. Indians, he said, sounding particularly supercilious, should always do *namaste.* The handshake was alien, improper, and a characterless imitation.

It made us bristle. In those days, politicians were not commonly disliked, but Desai left school a universally hated man. He had barely spent two hours on the campus, claiming he had to get back in time to greet Mrs Gandhi on her return from a foreign visit. We were only too happy to be rid of him.

A surprise, however, was to follow. When the next day's papers arrived, they carried front page photographs of Desai at the airport receiving Mrs Gandhi. And, what was he doing? He was shaking her hand!

Desai had tried to belittle the School but in the process, made himself seem small. Arun recognised the School's worth and visibly won us over. But I wonder if he noticed that it excels not just in the knowledge it teaches but, even more so, in the bigger wider lessons it encourages each boy to imbibe. On the day he visited, the boys sang Song No.3 from the School hymn book. It's by Iqbal, the man who first thought of Pakistan.

*Lab pe aati hei dua banke*
*Tamanna meri*
*Mere Allah burraie se*
*Bachanna mujhko*

As I joined in the singing, words long forgotten suddenly returning to memory in precise and perfect order, I recalled another truth about the School. At Doon, you know nothing of caste or communal division. Ram or Krishna, Allah or Christ, are the same. An Aggarwal and a Garg live side by side with a Rathore, a Vashisht, an Ahmed and a Henderson. And, they all have silly nicknames.

Could this be one Indian equivalent of Tasnim?

## *Amitabh, Naseer and Mummy*

The last rays of the sun were just starting to disappear behind the deodar trees as the play began. It was twilight and there was a distinct nip in the air. But there was enough light left to notice the apprehensiveness of the couple to my left. I was in the Rose Bowl at the Doon School and the play was an English translation of *Charandas Chor.* Their son, Imad, had a small part. There must have been several other parents feeling equally tense. Thirty years ago, mine too, would have had to grapple with similar emotions. But the pair beside me were a little special. They were Ratna and Naseeruddin Shah.

'Poor chap' I said, trying to make my voice soothing and my manner reassuring. 'Imad must be quite intimidated by your presence.'

'Not at all' Naseer laughed. 'I'm the one who's quivering and shaking!'

The play began slowly. That's not the sort of comment any of the watching parents would have made. In fact, if mine, way back in 1970, had said something like that I would have been mortally offended. Parents are meant to encourage and applaud. But I wasn't there as a parent, only as an old boy. And, this was the first time I was sitting in the audience watching a school play. On previous occasions, I had been part of the cast.

Yet, from the outset the mood of anticipation was clearly palpable. Everyone seemed to be anxiously waiting. The pace of the performance hardly mattered because the sense of expectation was so strong. But what was it, I asked myself, they were so keyed-up about? It reminded me of the audience at a production of *The Little Foxes* in London in 1984. On that occasion, everyone was sitting forward, craning their necks and struggling for a better view. Then, the explanation was simple. Elizabeth Taylor was playing the lead role. Here, at the Doon School, the answer eluded me until Naseer gave it away.

'There he is,' he suddenly whispered into my ear. 'In the *dhoti,* entering from the left. That's our son.'

When you have a son on stage, you don't need Elizabeth Taylor to excite you. The only difference was that the audience in London greeted Taylor's performance with loud *oohs* and *ahs*. At the Rose Bowl, the parents responded to their children with nervous little laughs followed, of course, with broad happy smiles. I'm afraid, I watched as much of Naseer and Ratna—albeit from the discreet corner of my eye—as I did of their son.

*Charandas Chor* took me back thirty-three years to April 1968. In the same Rose Bowl—practically on the same spot where last weekend Imad had stood—I recall the young Vikram Seth standing. In a captain's uniform, with a false moustache to make him look manly, he was playing the Chocolate Cream Soldier in Shaw's *Arms and the Man*. He was the star of the show and I had only a small insignificant part. But I was his nemesis. Engaged to the daughter of the house, he gets caught flirting with the maid. That was me. In those days, the boys of the Doon School, like early Roman actors, played all the parts in a play.

As Vikram embraced me, I was supposed to fall into his arms. It was, after all, seduction. But as he held me in a clinch—or whatever was permitted of one—my stockings started to roll down. As his ardour grew stronger, my legs slowly turned bare. By the time he had me in his grip, I looked more comic than alluring.

'Pull up your stockings, *yaar*,' someone shouted from the stands. Your peers can be merciless when you are twelve.

'Forget about her, Vikram,' said another voice. 'She's got hairy legs!'

This year, the Founder's Day chief guest was Amitabh Bachchan. I believe, I was the one who suggested his name but I could be wrong. Although there were some who thought otherwise, I feel it was an inspired choice. In previous years, the chief guests have been men of distinction: prime ministers, chief justices, prize-winning authors, even the Dalai Lama. Amitabh is equally distinguished, but he is also something more. He is popular. He was chosen not to please the teachers or the parents, but the boys.

Of that there can be little doubt. Long before he arrived, the whole of Dehra Dun knew he was coming. An hour before his car drove into School, the gates were shut to keep out the crowds. Inside, the Rose Bowl was crammed to capacity. There wasn't room to stand but there were still many who could not fit in. The overspill of several hundreds were seated on chairs outside, unable to see him in person but with access to a large screen replay.

For the Headmaster, who speaks first, it was a hard act to precede. Even the parents, who normally pay close attention to his annual report on the School's performance, were impatient to hear Mr Bachchan. And, the Chairman of the Board of Govs, who is next, knew he was only getting in the way.

So, when Amitabh got up to speak, he was heard in pin drop silence. I don't remember any shuffling of feet or crossing of legs. I don't recall hearing a single cough. And, yes, even the mobile phones seemed to go silent.

His rich, deep baritone filled the Rose Bowl. In response, a sea of smiling faces looked back at him. I'm sure, many did not pay attention to what he was saying. It was the power and impact of his delivery that mattered, or just the fact that he was there and speaking to them.

I tried to listen and there was a lot I liked about his speech. But unless I misheard him, there was one moment when I wondered if he really meant what he was saying.

'School days are the best days of your life,' he said repeating the old cliche, most boarding school students distrust. 'Cherish them and believe me, when I say, things get worse after this.'

He may be right, but isn't that a depressing message for teenagers to hear?

Sunday nights after Founder's Day are depressing. Each year, a pall of gloom descends over the Doon School. The festivities are over, your parents have gone and all that is left is the prospect of Monday morning school. I used to think of them as one of the worst nights of term and I can't believe the boys don't feel the same today.

In fact, what makes matters worse is that your parents always leave affecting an air of cheerfulness. My mother would depart smiling. I'd be close to tears but there wasn't even a hint of emotion in her voice. I used to think she was happy because she was leaving me behind.

This year, however, I saw Sunday night from the other side. On a train full of returning parents I realised how hard the wrench can be for them. It was their mobile phones that gave the secret away.

Normally, I disapprove of people who make pointless conversation on trains or planes. They have nothing to say, but nonetheless, say it ostentatiously. But last Sunday the conversations were a revelation.

'Hello *beta*,' I suddenly heard a voice say out loud. I turned to find my neighbour speaking. From the chord leading to his earpiece, I concluded he was talking into his phone. His face was sombre. His eyes were moist. His voice sounded heavy.

'So, son, three days are over and another Founder's Day is done. It was good to see you, *beta*.'

I couldn't hear what the son said but after a while, the father spoke again.

*'Hum Saharanpur pahunch gaye hein aur phir kuch ghantoon mein Dilli. Ab chutthi khattam aur kal office jana hei. Achcha nahin lag raha.'*

So, does that also mean Mummy's big smile and cheerful voice were put on?

## *Of priests and presidents*

A.P.J. Abdul Kalam reminds me of the man who married me, if you know what I mean! He was a Catholic priest from

Scotland. His name was Terry Gilfedder. Sadly, the last time we met was thirteen years ago. But I remember him clearly and the similarity is striking.

Last Saturday as I listened to the president, I could hardly believe what I was hearing. He was addressing the boys of the Doon School. It was the 67th Founder's Day and Dr Kalam was the chief guest. But the subject of his speech took me back twenty years to December 1982. The same thoughts—in fact, the same phrases—were also spoken then. But that was no school function, nor was I at the time a young boy. It was my marriage, Father Terry was the presiding priest and the words that came racing back to my mind, as I heard the president's speech, were from Father Terry's sermon.

President Kalam spoke of his recent visit to the Tawang Monastery. 'What advice can I take back for the people of India?' he asked the priests. Their answer was the subject of his Founder's Day address.

'Put aside violence,' they said. The priests are *Mahayana* Buddhists, famous for their *tankhas*. Forty years ago, they gave my father one, and it remains one of Mummy's prized possessions.

'And, how can we do that?' the president asked.

'By sublimating ego. It's ego that is the core of selfishness and from it stems all violence.'

'But how can this be done?' the president persisted. 'How can we control our egos?'

It was the answer to this question that took me back twenty years. Back to my own age of innocence and incomprehension; when you listen but don't necessarily understand.

'Learn to forget the I and the Me.' That was the answer. Simple, stark and short. I don't know how many of the four hundred and forty boys or their parents and guardians understood.

But when I heard the same words twenty years ago, I know I did not. As I sat listening to the president, on the main field of the Doon School, my mind flashed back to a small church in Nottinghill Gate, just off Westbourne Grove, on a bright December afternoon. There, Father Terry had said something similar.

'Karan and Nisha,' he said, pronouncing our names with the gentle lilt of his Scottish accent. 'I want to speak of three little words: I love you. Three words that symbolise today's ceremony and your relationship with each other. Love is the bond that unites you, but if you forget that you are two separate people, with separate habits, wishes and rights, love will also separate you. Never forget that you are two individuals and never let the I in you overrule the you of the other.'

Isn't it strange that two men, twenty years apart, one a catholic priest and the other the president of India, should have found words so reminiscent of each other to express a thought so simple, yet so difficult? Father Terry warned me against taking my wife for granted. President Kalam advised the boys of the Doon School against putting themselves first. But the point was the same. There is something beyond ourselves, as important if not more, and don't make yourself, your own ego, an obstacle reaching or understanding it.

I didn't heed Father Terry's wise counsel. To be honest, I did not fully understand him. Instead I laughed, as children often do, ridiculing what they cannot comprehend. I don't think the boys of the Doon School laughed. They are too polite, even too wise, for that. But perhaps, they were bemused. When you are sixteen, the 'I' is everything. At their age, and for many years afterwards, my world was Me and I was the centre of it.

Today at forty-six, I can see that other people matter because I have experienced how they do. That, I believe, is the catch.

I learnt to see beyond myself when I discovered how it could help me. This means, I learnt from my mistakes, from those dreadful knocks life deals each one of us, but that, sadly, is the only way one does. To be told is not enough. No priest and no president, no matter how sagely they advise or how seriously they warn, can make a difference.

Yet, they are right to try. And, do you know why? Because when your ego leads to your first fall and you start to nurse your bruises, it's the sudden flash-like memory of their words—may be long-forgotten but also starkly recalled—that helps you understand. It may be a lesson you don't heed but it's one you rarely forget. In need, it usually comes back.

## *When affection is a rude joke*

They say, there's nothing more cruel than schoolboys. They're wrong. Far worse are those you were at school with—even after thirty years! My class of 1971 at Doon had a re-union this weekend and I met up with several old friends I haven't seen for decades. But if anyone thought age, experience and wisdom would have curbed our penchant for laughter at someone else's expense—what I call digging it in—they couldn't have been more surprised.

'KT, just look at you!' was how I was greeted when I walked into the gathering. I soon discovered that the old school sobriquet was not used out of affection, so much as to emphasise the comment that was to follow. 'If your teeth are as white as your hair you could advertise Colgate!'

Less obvious, though no less pointed, was the second greeting with which I was accosted a short while later. This time, however, I required the full recall of my literary memory to understand!

'Hey!' said a familiar voice not heard since the early 1970s. I swivelled in its direction to find a group beckoning me. They were clearly enjoying themselves. 'Do you think you're Mary's little lamb?'

'What,' I spluttered, perplexed by the simile.

'Well, its fleece was white as snow and so is yours!'

Fortunately, they were tired of my hair fairly quickly. Unfortunately, that created the opening for jokes about my loquacity. To be honest, I don't think of myself as garrulous. But others do. Worse, my old school friends have also held firmly to the belief that I can't keep a secret. 'Telephone, telegram, tell Thapar,' was the saying when we were fifteen. As far as this lot is concerned, it holds good even today.

After a series of comments such as 'who thought Tota would join the Navy!' and '*yaar*, I can't believe monkey's become such a hot shot', attention turned to me. I knew I was in for another ribbing.

'KT, you chose the right profession.'

'Why?' I foolishly asked, falling into an obvious trap.

'Because you never let anyone talk in school. Now, as an anchor, you can keep on interrupting and claim you're doing your job!'

'In fact, why do you bother to have guests?' someone else butted in. He was smiling, but his tone was pure stiletto. 'The poor chaps don't get a word in edgeways. Why don't you call it "interview with self"? You know you'd love that'. To be honest, I would have been disappointed—actually upset—if our conversations hadn't started this way. Schoolboy affection is always disguised behind barbs and innuendo. It's less obvious but far sturdier than what you later encounter. In fact, I would add that you can always rely on someone whose leg you can pull. But can you equally trust a man you are formal with? Humour dissolves more than differences—it eliminates reserve, eradicates pomposity and obliterates the need for silly white lies.

I'm not sure if day school students can meet up after three decades with similar camaraderie, but I suspect not. On the other hand, the gruelling experience of a boarding school—and, of course, our capacity to romanticise memories, forgetting the dreadful whilst exaggerating the comic and peculiar—ensures that a friendship is never forgotten. Whilst you may not meet for years—even decades—and that was true of many of the class of 1971—when you do, you can strike a chord instantaneously. And, even if the rekindled old flame may start to flicker and fade after a bit, it will certainly shine brightly for the duration of a re-union.

Wellington was only slightly incorrect when he claimed that the Battle of Waterloo was won on the playing fields of Eton. I suspect the roots of that victory more accurately stretch back to the pranks played in the dormitories, the punishments inflicted by prefects and the homework hastily completed with a little help from the class egghead minutes before submission. Such incidents may or may not have put iron in the Duke, but for the rest of us, they've promoted self-reliance, self-confidence and an ability to see the funny side of any predicament. What's more, they've forged bonds that have survived the test of time.

So, even if school days are not the best in your life—and, actually, it would be rather sad if they were—the boarding school experience is undoubtedly special. But you have to know it to truly understand why.

## *Are Tolstoy and Gupta saying the same thing?*

There is a Tolstoy short story that was a favourite when I was at school. It was my introduction to the great author and I well remember it. Called 'How much land does a man need?' I did not fully understand it when I first read it. At the time I thought it pointless. But now, I realise how clever it is.

If I am correct, it is about an offer with a catch. Land is being given away and any of the claimants can have as much as they can circumscribe by running around it. The condition is, you have to return to the point whence you started, before the sun sets.

The protagonist, if my memory isn't faulty, covers a vast circumference. His aim is to claim as much land as he possibly can. As he heads back, he can see the sun setting. It's delicately poised, and he races desperately to return before it disappears below the horizon. Against all the odds he makes, it but at his moment of triumph, his effort kills him.

Instead of claiming the hundreds of acres he has run around, he's buried in six feet of ground. How much land does a man need?

It took me years to appreciate that the story is about the self-destroying consequences of human greed. Happiness lies in contentment with what you have or, at least, what you can use. More than that is not only pointless, it is meaningless. But it can also be self-destructive.

Well, last week Tolstoy's story—I must have been eleven or twelve when I first encountered it at The Doon School—came rushing back in imperfect detail as I read Dipankar Gupta's latest book. It's called *Mistaken Modernity*, and the chapter on the nature of Indian politicians raises the question 'how many free phone calls does an MP require?'

After pointing out that last year—or, was it this year? they do this sort of thing so often one can be forgiven the confusion—MPs gifted themselves a hundred thousand free phone calls a year, he calculates what this actually means.

> 'One lakh telephone calls would mean roughly 275 calls a day. Assuming a 12-hour waking cycle for MPs, that would mean about twenty-three calls an hour. If each call lasts for about three minutes, their diurnal clock has already run out of sand. This is literally an embarrassment of riches.'

To be able to utilise all the free phones they have granted themselves, MPs would have precious little time for anything else. Perhaps, that might be a blessing because they would, as a result, have no time left to interfere in our lives. But this simple statistic does suggest that Dipankar's view of politics is unimpeachable. Let me share it with you.

> 'It is true that there are a large number of corrupt people in Indian politics. But what is equally true is that a large number of people join politics, so that they can become corrupt.... This is because politics alone offers the average Indian a chance of getting rich quick and climbing up the social ladder within a lifetime. The demand for clean politics is thus defeated at the very root.'

Reflect a little on Dipankar's views this Sunday morning: are our MPs greedy or do my recollections of Tolstoy mislead me?

## *Au revoir Ashraf*

I was staring absent-mindedly out of the window when a colleague asked a question which sparked off a chain of thoughts. News of Ashraf Qazi's recall had just been announced and although I had anticipated it, I was still a little shaken. Even when something is inevitable, you hope it won't happen. This was certainly one such occasion.

'Are you upset?' Ashok asked.

I suppose, the look on my face gave me away. But until he asked the question, I did not realise that this was the emotion inside me. I had not paused to consider how I felt. It seemed irrelevant to the larger events happening outside. But now that Ashok had drawn my attention to my feelings, I knew he was right.

Ashraf was a friend I got to know five years ago. Before that, I only knew him as Abidah's husband. In fact, on the one previous occasion that we met—in Islamabad in 1989—he seemed stiff; an impression so wrong, its only purpose is to underline how little I knew him before 1997.

Over the last five years, we became close friends. I found him warm, supportive, trusting and loyal. He was a *bon viveur,* the soul of dinner parties with a manner that put people instantly at ease. If ever a Pakistani knew how to take the sting out of a tense situation, it was Ashraf. But the nicest thing was that he combined two welcome but contradictory qualities: a sharp intelligence with a delightful appetite for good-natured gossip.

Two years ago, he pushed to get me an interview with General Musharraf. By coincidence, we flew to Pakistan together. Ashraf was returning to visit his mother.

'How did it go?' he asked the night it happened.

'Okay,' I replied non-committally. I knew he would not like it but I did not know how to say that. I also knew that the response in India would be different, but I did not want to say that either.

Five days after the interview was broadcast, Ashraf returned. The next morning he telephoned.

'You know I thought you'd done me in,' he began but he was laughing. 'My heart sank when I saw the interview. Then, I read the *Times of India* and thank God, for their silly criticism. I don't agree with them but they may have saved my job!'

Any other High Commissioner would have taken the matter far more seriously. It could have broken our friendship. Not Ashraf. We went on to become better and closer friends.

A few months later, we spent a weekend together in Dehra Dun and Mussoorie. It was The Doon School's Founder's Day and I thought Ashraf ought to see our best school. We drove down together in his Mitsubishi. On the way back, he was determined to see Haridwar and Rishikesh. For a while, I lost him in the crowd at Lakshman Jhula but when I found him again, he was beaming with delight.

'What's up?' I asked.

'You know that lovely tune we heard in the Mall in Mussoorie? I just bought it.'

'What tune?' I hadn't the faintest idea what he was talking about.

'You're a twit. Wait, till I put it on.'

As we drove off, he inserted the tape in the car deck and turned to look at me as it started to play. It was Jagjit Singh's *Ram Dhun*.

'Remember it?'

I could not. I had not heard it as we walked up the Mussoorie Mall. Yet, Ashraf's ears had picked it up. He had liked it and now, he had made a point of buying it. We drove back listening to the tape. Each time it ended, he would rewind and start again.

Last December, the day I was leaving for a brief new year break in London, Ashraf telephoned at lunch time.

'Let's have a bite together,' he suggested.

'I can't. I'm in a dreadful rush and besides, you know I hate lunch.'

'Yes, I know. But we may never meet again. The way things are developing, I may be gone before you return.'

We spent a couple of hours at the Taj Coffee Shop and I can't remember laughing as much on any other occasion. His heart was heavy because he did not want to leave but no one would have realised that. Initially, even I did not. Fortunately, on that occasion his fears were mistaken. Not this time. I was the one who first predicted last Friday that his time was up. He instantly agreed.

Yesterday, Ashraf went back to Pakistan but I hope it will only be for a short stay. Officially, he's just been recalled. Formally, he remains the Pakistan High Commissioner to India. I pray our relations improve in time for him to return.

## *Dreaming with Kuchipuddi*

It's reassuring when people don't change. They may grow up, get fat or become old but when the core of their personality stays the same, you still feel you know them. That's how I felt when I met Amitav Ghosh last weekend. Ten years had lapsed since our last contact. In theory, therefore, we were meeting like strangers. But Amitav's unchanged manner immediately rekindled the old relationship. It was as instant as coffee.

'Currybins,' he roared, his face smiling broadly. When it does, his eyes disappear behind rising cheekbones. His voice approaches a falsetto.

'Kuchipuddi,' I replied recalling the name I gave him at school.

We laughed uproariously. Those who witnessed our re-union, must have marvelled at two middle-aged white-haired men, laughing helplessly for no discernible reason, other than they were meeting after a long time.

Instinctively, we reverted to nicknames that go back a quarter century. They were last used, sitting on the steps of the school pavilion. It was a cold December night, the last before I left Doon. Amitav still had a year to go. This was our farewell. Of course, we insisted, we would keep in touch but perhaps, intuitively we knew how unlikely that would be. Time had proved that intuition correct. Yet, by using the old sobriquets a bridge had formed across the divide.

Since I last knew him, Amitav has become one of the finest Indian authors in English. The physical change is equally striking. The younger Amitav had a dishevelled bohemian air. His hair was always undone. Today, his white mop contrasts sharply with his deep brown skin. The effect is at once distinguished and dramatic. It arrests your attention. But he has not lost his habit of looking at you through the sides of his eyes. He does it most often, when he's smiling. It gives him a mischievous schoolboy look.

We were meeting for an interview. Amitav was my guest. That meant I had to 'find out' about him, read the cuttings, research, talk to his friends. I was surprised by how little I knew. For instance, I had no idea his had been a quiet, even a lonely, childhood. The garrulous, often loquacious, teenager I remembered seemed anything but solitary.

'I was an avid reader,' he began. 'That's partly to do with my childhood. I grew to distrust the outside world and created my own.'

He was twelve when he read Sholokhov's *Quiet Flows the Don.* It was a gift from an uncle and perhaps, his first serious book. Years later, he discovered a handful of authors who started similarly. Sholokhov's novel was the link between them. But was it also the secret of their success? I warned Amitav that if he said yes, thousands of eager parents might rush to buy copies and their children would not thank him for this infliction. He laughed. 'Serves them right.'

I had read that Amitav wrote his first book, *The Circle of Reason,* in a hot, sweaty *barsati* in Defence Colony. Was this the Indian equivalent of an artist's garret in Montmartre?

'Actually, it was a servant's quarter!' he laughed. 'Do you know, as I was sitting there sweating in the *barsati* I used to think that some day someone is going to ask me that!'

The book is an enchanting journey into the head of its protagonist, a character fondly called Aloo. What I did not know is that the published version is the second draft. The first was discarded.

'It took me an year to write but by the time I read ten pages I knew it was awful,' he revealed. 'I took all the work, all three hundred pages, and threw it away!'

He began all over again. Amitav gave himself an year but decided if nothing came of it, he would reconsider his dream of becoming a writer.

'So, a point of desperation had been reached?'

'I think that kind of desperation, that sense that your life depends on it, either the book will kill you or you'll be able to write a book, that's what puts life into a book.'

Fortunately, the second draft survived. It didn't win instant recognition but secured a firm foothold and he's been climbing ever since. Today, he's deservedly successful but the fire and passion have not dimmed. Writing is all he wants to do. Yet, he marvels at how far it's taken him.

'I've a sense of wonderment,' he exclaimed. 'To think that my books go out in the world and send back these ripples is for me, in a sense, completely miraculous. I feel amazed by my life. I feel amazed by what happens to me.'

'Do you think it's a dream and you'll wake up to find it's not true?' 'That's the nightmare I often have.'

### *A felicitous encounter*

It's odd how one thing leads to another. London brought back memories of The Doon School. The cause of this flashback was the matinee I saw last Saturday. It was rather appropriately called *Alarms and Excursions.*

London is the home of the world's best theatre and a visit to the wicked city without this little indulgence would not be complete. Sadly, this autumn, most of the fare on offer is old musicals. Although the National Theatre's revival of *Oklahoma* is superb, you can't even steal a ticket. So, I settled for the new Michael Frayn comedy starring Felicity Kendall.

Let me reveal a secret. I have a soft spot for this incredible actress. Long, long before the BBC made her famous in *The Good Life*, the Doon School introduced her to its students as the young prince in *Hamlet.* And, what a comely little boy she was to boot!

In those days, with a packed audience of pubescent teenagers staring at her leotard-covered legs, she would stand upright on the stage. As we watched with our mouths wide open, she would lift one of the rickety old school chairs whilst her father, Geoffrey Kendall, whose voice could boom like quadraphonic music, would proclaim: 'In Shakespeare's day, the stage was bare. The throne of Denmark was but a chair.'

Those silly lines were enough to send the school into peals of laughter. But the lucky ones in the front row, with a felicitous view of Miss Kendall's legs, were too engrossed in her beauty to be so easily distracted. I was a habitual front-rower and my attention never strayed.

The year was 1966, I was ten and I fell in love with Felicity. So did half the school. In the decades to follow, Shashi Kapoor married her sister, Jenniffer, and Felicity went on to become perhaps, the most versatile theatre actress of our time. But the childhood flame was never quite doused.

Last Saturday, as I watched her—and despite the poor quality of the play—the embers rekindled. Once again, I was in the front row but this time I didn't try and stare up her skirt. Instead, I sat mesmerised by her talent.

Now, if you've only seen our Bollywood heavies prancing on artificial sets in heaving costumes and excessive make-up, then you can have no way of imagining the impact of good acting. Like magic, it transports you into another world. It takes you out of yourself into another level of consciousness.

To think that Doscos in the 1960s should have experienced this with the young Felicity would make English minds boggle. What is even harder to credit is that, she learnt her trade in the damp and smelly green rooms of Indian public schools. But then, truth is often stranger than fiction.

Oddly enough, you used to get the best ice cream at The Doon School. It was made in large hard-turned wooden vats and was creamy, yet light. But that was a long long time ago. Today, good ice cream is difficult to find. So, here's a spot of good news.

If you're fond of decent ice cream, I have a tip for you. Drive down Lodhi Road to the petrol station beside the HUDCO building, park your car in the shade and head straight for the little shop. Walk past the cash counter, avoiding the biscuits and jams, all the way to the far end and open the freezer marked Movenpick. It's Swiss ice cream and it's delicious. It is one of my favourites and I had not expected to find it in Delhi, leave aside in a petrol station. But it's here and let's hope it stays.

There are three flavours to choose from of which, I believe, the capuccino is the best. But if you prefer strong tastes, then try the strawberry yoghurt, or even the chocolate chip.

Last Sunday, they were doling out free samples to taste. I'm not sure if that will be the case today. But if you decide to try your luck, keep a 50-rupee note handy. That's what it will cost, in case you're asked to pay.

# The 'Doon' Syndrome

Dev Lahiri

Mohd Ra'ab or 'Ra'ab Sahib', as he was popularly known, was a 'Mafia don' in Kolkata in the late 1980s. Now, what has this got to do with the tradition of education in the Doon Valley, you may well ask. Well, let me tell you this little story first.

I was in Kolkata for the X-mas holidays in the December of 1988, as a young master in the Doon School. A friend of mine visited me one evening at my in-laws' with whom I was staying, with a very worried look on his face.

'You have to do me a big favour,' he said. 'And, please don't say no.'

'What is it, and why are you looking so distraught?' I asked.

'It's like this. Ra'ab sahib is very anxious to meet you, and has asked me to take you along for dinner to his place. Please, don't refuse.'

To cut a long story short, I visited 'Ra'ab sahib'; what I saw and experienced during that visit, I shall save for another occasion, but the reason why this powerful 'Don' wanted to see me was simple—'*Ladke ko Doon mein padana hai* (I have to educate my son in Doon)'. This was, he explained to me, the wish of a father who knew that his days were numbered!

And so, it is with thousands of others. Just as scores of young men and women head for Mumbai with dreams of seeing themselves on posters, so also hordes of eager parents arrive in Dehra Dun each year, full of hopes and aspirations for their children. For most of them, the act of sending their ward to 'Doon' is the end of the search for the Holy Grail. It does not matter, whether the school is 'Doon Public', or 'Doon International' or 'Doon Boys'—or indeed, any institution either prefixed or suffixed by those four magic letters—DOON. If it's Doon, it's got to be good! There are, at the moment, approximately, a staggering 700-odd schools in the Dehra Dun–Mussoorie belt!

Whence and why this 'boom' of schools in this area? What drives all these parents to the valley, in their quest to give their children the 'best'? A large part of the answer lies undeniably in the mere presence of The Doon School. And by this, I mean the original Doon School. Founded in 1935, The Doon School has, over the years, come to epitomise the best in good educational practices—at least, as far as Public Schools are concerned. Moreover, the school has a list of alumni that would put any 'Who's Who' to shame. The popularity of this 'Doon Syndrome' perhaps, reached its peak in 1985, when during the Golden Jubilee celebrations of the school, the nation suddenly woke up to the fact that the then Prime Minister Rajiv Gandhi was also an alumnus. Rajiv Gandhi was the glittering star—the role model that every upwardly mobile middle-class Indian wanted his son to emulate. What has happened over the years is that 'willy-nilly', the distinction between sending your son to The Doon School, and sending him to the Doon Valley, has become very blurred. After all, if you are to say in Lalu country, '*Mera Beta Doon mein padta hain*' (my son studies in Doon), who is to know the difference?

Of course, there are other factors, too. The Doon Valley has traditionally been associated with natural beauty, a clean environment, ideal climatic conditions, huge playing fields—in short, the ideal conditions to bring up a child. Add to this, a huge networking of schools, and you could not ask for more!

But all this is now being seriously challenged. Education has become a seriously competitive business. It is not good enough to flaunt the 'Doon' label. A school must be able to convince its clientele that it has a motivated, well-trained faculty, up with the latest educational techniques, state-of-the-art infrastructure, and of course, excellent results. Moreover, Dehra Dun is no longer the environmental paradise it once was. Ugly high-rise buildings, pollution, traffic, unplanned growth and rising crime, all continue to effectively destroy the great advantage that the Doon Valley once had. So, schooling in Dehra Dun is now just 'limping along'.

A pity, really, considering the hoary traditions and culture that schools have bequeathed to this valley many an ex-student will regale his children, and perhaps grandchildren, with stories of his exploits whilst at school here. Some of these stories are almost legendary. Such as the one about the Housemaster who crept into the bed of a ward who had sneaked out for a late-night movie, and fell blissfully asleep. Imagine the shock felt by the errant lad, when he sleepily tumbled into his bed, to find his Housemaster snoring beside him! Then, there is that story of some students in a boarding school who surreptitiously ordered a meal for themselves from a local restaurant. The understanding was, that the 'feast' was to be delivered at a clandestine location, near a breach in the boundary wall. Unfortunately, things got a little mixed up. The delivery boy had to be changed at the last minute, and the new man delivered the food to the Headmaster's residence, instead! Thereupon, the enterprising and somewhat bemused Housemaster, organised a party for the staff that evening!

Tales such as these abound, along with memories of immortal teachers. The legendary Holdsworth of The Doon School (or 'Holdie' as he is popularly known), Mr Marshall, who reputedly knew every single child who went through his hands by name, Mr Tuck of Cambrian Hall, 'Charlie' Kandhari of Welham Boys, Misses Linnell & Oliphant—the list of these colossuses who left an indelible stamp, both on the institution and the children they were associated with, is endless.

So, what happens to all that now? Does it become consigned to the dustbin of history? Not really, because those generations that have gone through the magic of a 'Doon' education (and I use the word in the sense of the valley), can never really forget their years here or, indeed, the impact that those years have had on their lives.

But the Doon Valley has to respond to all these challenges, and at the moment, these responses are somewhat knee-jerk. A whole host of private entrepreneurs have now stepped in, in order to try and redress the perceived shortcomings of the 'old-fashioned' schools. The buzzword is to call yourself an 'International' or 'World' School, and much to the horror of the old well-heeled schools, launch an advertising blitz! So, Dehra Dun is seeing what it has never seen before—giant hoardings that advertise schools, TV commercials, pages of ads in the 'classified'—you name it, they do it!

But, has this led to a quantum leap forward in the quality of education on offer? It is early days yet, but judging by the reactions of several parents who have opted for the 'new-wave' schools, the answer seems to be 'No'. To begin with, good teachers are at a premium in the entire country, and the problem is doubly exacerbated in Dehra Dun, which is not really in a position to attract the best talent. Moreover, the teachers who do find themselves lured by the glossy ads, soon discover that money can never be a substitute for positive, encouraging, working conditions.

The problem, as an old resident pointed out, is that most of the new schools are in it for the money. Delivering education is a secondary objective. Take the case of a well-known 'World School' that was inaugurated in 2002. As of date, it has changed four principals and over eighty teachers!

Along with the mushrooming of these new schools, Dehra Dun is also witnessing an explosion, as far as professional institutions are concerned. There are institutes of technology, fashion design, for training air-hostesses, graphic designers—the list is mind-boggling. The streets are full of smartly-clad young men and women in natty uniforms, exuding oodles of self-confidence and belief. A welcome change, no doubt, from the old days, when all one saw of post-school youth was youngsters hanging around purposelessly at Astley Hall and a few select areas on Rajpur Road. What kind of career opportunities these young people will be able to avail of, still remains to be seen. But given the booming economy, there is every reason to hope.

And, hope we must, as Dehra Dun undergoes this metamorphoses and finds itself catapulted into the New Age. At the end of the day, each institution will have to take a call on how much of the old and how much of the new it wishes to synergise. The young men and women who emerge from these institutions have the unenviable task of setting right the wrongs of their predecessors. Will they be good enough? Only time will tell.

In the meanwhile, Dehra Dun continues to be a happy hunting ground for liquor-barons, hoteliers, politicians, property tycoons—in short, anyone with pots of spare money looking for a good investment opportunity and the reputation of an 'educationist' to boot! After all, in this country, all you need is a formal schooling (and sometimes, not even that) to qualify (if you wish to be invited to address symposiums on education) as an 'educationist'! All you need to do is to get on to the net and pick up some jargon. If, however, you are modest in your ambitions, that too is not necessary.

This infusion of 'buccaneers' into the staid old-fashioned educationist environment of Dehra Dun is bound to have a ripple effect on the rest of society as well. To begin with, in order to recover costs on investments, the doors of these institutions have been thrown open to anyone who can pay. Gone are the days of strict entrance examinations, transparent admission procedures, and checks on candidates' backgrounds. Now, political patronage, bureaucratic clout and, most importantly, deep pockets call the shots. Little wonder then that, the director of a private medical college was shot at, and grievously injured, by two students he had rusticated. And, this is the same Doon Valley where the Headmaster of The Doon School could once imperiously tell Pandit Nehru that his grandson was not entitled to an outing on that particular weekend! Raab-Sahib (May his soul rest in peace after the last police encounter) is probably blessing his stars that his son never made it to a school in Doon.

# The East Canal

Irwin Allan Sealy

It's buried now and gone, as most Dehra canals are. But fresh from Amsterdam, city of canals, home just yesterday from those tranquil waterways, I want to exhume the East Canal.

It needn't have died. With a little imagination Dehra Dun's oldest canal could have been saved. With a little hard work, we could have learned to keep it clean.

'But the Dutch are clean,' you point out, 'we're *not*. Look at our streets.'

'Look at their sinks,' I agree, arguing against myself. The sink in my very ordinary hotel room shone like the evening star.

But if you could have seen the old canal of my childhood, even the canal of ten years ago, you would have sworn it was worth saving. It sparkled like the costliest bottled water in the world, and it ran free. Clear water, sweet water, running fresh and swift from the lowest Himalayas, it visited the town to speak its benediction, and flashed back out into the fields to the south, spent. So, it served two purposes, supplying the city's waterworks and irrigating the valley's rice paddies and kitchen gardens.

I call it the East Canal but properly the stretch I knew and still treasure was the Dharampur branch of the Rajpur Canal, first of Dehra Dun's man-made channels. It just happened to run alongside what I knew as East Canal Road and the road's name stuck to the canal, perhaps, in no one else's head but mine. To me it was the equal of the Roman aqueduct at Nimes.

Waterworks are markers of civilisation. In our city we have committed three recent crimes, small but significant crimes, against hydraulic civilisation. We destroyed the East Canal and are destroying others. We razed a happy little watermill on the same canal at Survey Chowk, a mill that was functioning in my childhood, and a piece of history that any other city in the world would have been proud to restore, even as a shell, letting traffic flow around it. And, we are killing by neglect Shore's Well, a listed monument, the city's first deep well, over two hundred feet deep, a magnificent covered structure from the 1820s, that huddles in ruins behind the law courts, with pipal trees growing out of its dome. (If you wanted to add 3(a): we have put up ugly concrete water towers on the public *maidan*, the only lungs of the city, a space where no permanent structure of any kind is permitted by statute.)

It would make a nice change from television to see the men responsible for these atrocities paraded on some Sunday, perhaps, on the same maidan before the afternoon's wrestling, on donkeys. But anonymity is the rule of engineering, civil and uncivil, so let us instead, honour those who built well.

The Rajpur Canal is said to follow the route of a seventeenth century canal built for Queen Karnavati of nearby Nawada; the gifted Najib Khan of Saharanpur was another of its patrons. Agriculture in this valley flourished under those capable rulers. In the 1840s, British surveyors and engineers, prominent among them, Captain Cautley, later knighted for his work on the Ganges Canal, revived the moribund *nala* as part of a larger project involving some hundreds of miles of valley irrigation channels.

There was the canal I remember. Hemmed in with square-cut blocks of grey stone, hedged by tussock and reeds and wildflowers, it flowed past our Dalanwala house with great energy. The gradient was steep and every half mile or so, the canal widened into a well where the water fell with a great to-do, churning and frothing for an interval, as if mulling over some sinister plot. These wells were objects of every child's fascination and dread: if the falls did that to your paper boat, what might they choose do to you? And, you stepped back warily from the brink. But it was impossible to go far: little by little you edged in again to follow the canal as it found its new level and swept along once more. Presently, you left the thunder behind and were drawn by a new and even more hypnotic danger, an aching stillness. In such passages of clarity and silence the water was hung with streamers of olive green weed that beckoned slyly to you as you trod on cushions of slippery moss. 'Come sleep!' they whispered, 'just fall asleep!' Was it really moving, was it *water* at all, or was it a crystal medium into which you could slip effortlessly and never wish to return? Liquid music, the magic of it was that it could never end.

Five years ago it ended. That summer of 2002, a deep trench was dug alongside the canal, wide bore concrete pipes appeared and were lowered into it and joined up, and the water was diverted into them and disappeared underground forever. For the first time in a century and a half, the canal bed was laid bare. I took my friend, Palash to inspect the ruins. Already, workers were dismantling the old structure and stone blocks lay about in heaps on either side of the dry watercourse. At the bottom of E.C. Road, where there were more nineteenth century remains, either a police *chowki* or another mill (also since demolished), the old canal went under the road. We climbed down into the culvert and took a dismal photo. It looks like a tomb, and it is. I have photos of Mayan burial chambers that look jollier. My 1959 Fiat, relic of a brighter decade, stands witness to the desolation.

It was inevitable, everyone said. All those plastic bags. People were throwing their rubbish in the canal, the city fathers said; it had become too hard to maintain. And, it is true I saw a woman empty her dustbin into its clear water, as if this were any of our reliable and long-suffering rivers. She was a poor woman, but it's a myth that the poor are the only polluters. (In middle class Race Course, people think nothing of leaving an uprooted toilet seat right outside their gate, where it will lie unnoticed, because it has passed beyond that sacred line of visibility, the boundary wall.) Presented with the facts, and shown alternatives, rich and poor could have mobilised against the destruction; democracy must not only permit right action but encourage it. And, both classes are changing with incalculable speed. Well it's gone, but if historical monuments are a luxury, (they're not, of course) then I hope in the India of a hundred years from now, engineers will reconstruct the canal for a prosperous citizenry. Alas, when they do, they will find a small chunk missing, in the shape of a harp seat.

A harp seat? Read on.

After our first recce things moved quickly and slowly, as always. Every time I drove up E.C. Road, or rode my Kinetic

Spark down it, there were gangs of men taking the remains apart. They worked with crowbar and pickaxe and camped on the site. Their tents and charpoys sprawled over the old embankment, their hookahs and campfires glowed in the dark; the night air smelt of dust and tobacco and fresh *rotis*. By day, tractor trolleys appeared, were loaded with soil and driven off. Dust flew, pedestrians picked their way over random humps of newly packed earth, traffic raced past raising still more dust. In a little while, the green fringe of my childhood was gone.

It was then I had my notion.

I picked up a block of stone. It was not especially heavy but it was not light. Say, five bricks' weight. The blocks were of various sizes and not all were truly squared off. You had to pick and choose and even then, a round underside could surprise you. I chose one that looked roughly cubic. It must have weighed 10 kilos, possibly a little more. I laid it flat on the running board of the Kinetic, which sank a millimetre but made no complaint. I kick-started and rode off down E.C. Road.

Over the next month, I returned frequently to the plunder. Seldom did a day go by without a kill. I would target a likely piece, stroll up and down whistling, and when all backs were turned, strike. I grew ambitious, eyeing ever bigger rocks: it was hard on the heart. I had to work fast, too. The rock-breakers were now at work, reducing the hewn stone to bedrock metal for the road-widening. Some nights, I made two trips. Once, I brought the Fiat and took five stones at one go, setting in train a whole new riff of palpitations. The doctor shook his head, my mason boggled, my wife rolled her eyes up to heaven. But the pile grew. Then, I unveiled my plan: a stone garden seat, crescent-shaped, strung with bands of iron of diminishing lengths, like a harp of old.

We set to work, the mason and I; we build everything together. The harp seat would be my memorial to the lost waters. By the time it was ready, not a trace was left of the East Canal.

Since that time a larger peril has arisen. A far greater canal is in danger. Not that you could bury this one. The Ganges Canal is one of the monuments of world engineering. Up to the end of the nineteenth century, it was the greatest irrigation canal in the world. Today, it winds hundreds of kilometres through the green fields and orchards of two states, Uttarakhand and Uttar Pradesh. The road to Delhi crosses it twice and every time I pass, I lean out of the bus window to gaze upon the placid waterway. Surrounded by fields, bordered with trees far as the horizon, it moves at its own pace and keeps its counsel. Muddy as a river, and as broad, but without a river's bends and wrinkles, its smooth face is always unreadable; its eyes never meet yours, as if its whole dialogue were with the sky. Winter or summer, it is the most peaceful vision you could hope for, and every time it leaves me on the verge of tears. Here, as nowhere else I know, do the worlds of man and nature meet without war.

Now, imagine a six-lane highway alongside the canal. Because that is the plan. There are existing highways between Delhi and Dehra Dun that could be widened, but the planners have lit on this route. Funds have been sanctioned; I'm told, work has begun.

I'm not asking for a return to the bullock cart. The Dehra Dun–Delhi road via Saharanpur, already a fine and motorable road, could very easily be widened to serve the same purpose. And, the canal left alone to wind its peaceful way through some of the finest cropland in the country. If revenue is a concern, we could even conduct barge tours along it and find quiet takers here and abroad. After all, navigation was the other, and equal, brief of the builders. It's a thought. This is not the East Canal: the whole world is watching. While we're about it, we could replace the picturesque rutted track on either side with a decent road for local cyclists and carts. But not a freeway. (A better train link with the capital we do need, and more—and faster—trains; the present six hours over 250 kilometres is a little sad in the twenty-first century. Let the slow route be the canal.) There are many alternatives, and the reasons given by the freeway lobby don't add up.

Of course, there are other modes of human transportation, and one of these came home to me in Holland. I did no sightseeing during my week there, none at all, but it was my pleasure every day to sit and watch the people, and more than anything else, to watch them ride. The Dutch are the world's greatest bicyclists. Not the fastest or the mightiest (those are precisely the kinds of categories—beloved of the French, the Japanese, the Americans—this remarkable people distrust), just the most enthusiastic, the most benign, in short the best. '*Look! Look!!*' a Dutchman sang out when I jaywalked and strayed into his path, almost causing an accident. Another race would have cursed me roundly, and I deserved it, pretending I was a local. Such a tolerant, courteous, humane people! So open (their curtains tellingly undrawn at night), unbuttoned, and practical that every Indian could learn something from them.

The least abstract lesson would be the simplest: a bicycle lane on our roads. And yes, I have a particular road in mind. East Canal Road. None of the usual excuses our city fathers trot out obtains here. It is straight enough and level enough and, thanks to their encroachment, it is wide enough. Let the track be no wider than the old canal. A single metre-wide lane dedicated to bicycles. Let it be on the east side of the road. And, let it run right above the buried canal. The dark waters would rejoice in their depths.

I already have a bicycle picked out and will be among the first riders. My daughter, quicker off the mark, will pass us coming back. And, who knows, paid-up Gandhians, anarchists, and members of the revolutionary middle class would join those who ride not for pleasure but because they're going somewhere. We might even mark the spot at Survey Chowk where the old watermill stood and name it in honour of Queen Karnavati, if she would stoop to milling flour. The East Canal Bicycle Track would be a fitter memorial than mine of the stolen rocks, and I hope more enduring.

I have a last confession. Five years on, the harp seat still lacks the inscription I intended to justify it. A set of cold chisels especially forged for the occasion by a friend with a steel works still has its virginal edge. But the carving will come, maybe, as soon as the putting down of this pencil. I'm getting sick of writing. When it does, the keystone will bear a simple legend in Roman capitals:

IM
EC

I spell it out for those who call me cryptic. *In Memoriam East Canal.*

# Last Train to Dehra Dun

Victor Banerjee

My name is, or should I say, was? No. Let's not confuse issues for the moment. My name is Trilok. I have just boarded the Mussoorie Express at New Delhi's Old Delhi station and am on my way home to Kanda gaon. No, the train doesn't go there. It stops at Dehra Dun. I have to take a two-hour bus ride to Mussoorie in the mountains and then walk to Lal Tibba, in Landour, from where you can see my village, and even my house in the valley below, under the snow-capped peaks of Gangotri and Bandarpunch in the horizon, that you can almost reach out and touch.

Two years ago, I suffered a mild stroke that left me with slightly slurred speech and a weak leg. Walking down the narrow mountain path to my village would now take at least four hours, compared to the hour it used to take me before I fell ill. If the train gets in on time, I should make it to the top of the mountain on time to catch up with my friend Uday on his way back home, after delivering milk to various people on the hillside and the sweet shops in Landour bazaar. He was my age and would help me to make sure I got home safe and sound, before nightfall.

I have left my job in Greater Kailash, or G.K. as the Delhiwallahs call it. I had worked for the Mehras for twenty-seven years. Five nights ago, their daughter Pinky, whom I had at one time cradled in my arms and escorted to primary school, and for whom I had often stood in long lines to purchase tickets on the first day of a Jeetendra or Shahrukh release, and even slept many many nights on the doormat outside to quietly let her in when she returned from all-night parties with friends, got engaged to the son of a doctor from New Friends Colony, Dr Amar Yadav, famous for expensive and discreet abortions. He had bailed out many a morally bankrupt hero who thought he could ride roughshod over peoples' deprived circumstances and get away with it. They did. The doctor's boy's name was Sunny.

As the evening progressed, Sunny and his father had got more and more drunk and boisterous and Pinky, poor girl, grew more and more troubled and embarrassed. Sunny would suddenly appear out of nowhere, grab Pinky, by the arm and rudely shoving elders and ladies, and anyone else who stood in his way aside, would drag her across the room to meet one or another of his tacky college buddies who were as drunk as he was. They would all leer lasciviously at Pinky while she squirmed in discomfort. When she blushed and looked away, they rubbed their crotches and made rude and crude gestures that Sunny, grinning through stained teeth and an alcoholic's froth around his mouth, coarsely enjoyed. That's when it happened.

Pinky noticed that an emerald and diamond bangle that Sunny's father had presented her that evening, was missing from her wrist. Within seconds, all hell broke loose and the father-and-son-duo turned loud, vicious and abusive, as they looked around for people they could accuse of stealing the bracelet. Stagnantly mobile Delhiites, incapable of comprehending anything besides investments in real estate and the decilitre measure of a drink served in parking lots from bars set in cars' dickeys under blinking taillights, were unruffled.

I walked out of the pantry to see what the racket was all about and saw Pinky sobbing with her face covered in her hands and Sunny screaming, for the son-of-a-bitch who had stolen the bracelet to own up now, or else. I felt a solid thump at the back of my neck. My leg gave in and I collapsed onto the floor.

Stunned and scared, I looked up to see Sunny's father standing over me and I heard shouts of 'This bastard. Can't be anyone else', till I felt a piercing pain in my side and almost blacked out. Sunny had walked up and kicked me with his steel-tipped crocodile-skin-embossed shoe. Someone grabbed my collar and someone else my hair and I was pulled up off the floor. But no sooner than I had straightened up than I was again punched in the face by Sunny and kicked in the stomach, while I crumpled to the floor.

I spent that night in jail. In the lock-up, with two seasoned thieves, freezing on a cold cement floor. The blood on my brow had dried. My arthritic knee felt like it had been twisted out of its socket. Laboni, a kind and scarred illegal Bangladeshi immigrant, who had recently been hired by the Mehra's as a cook, told me later that Pinky had wept to see me being dragged off by the police who kicked me down the stairs and into the street, all the while hitting me ruthlessly on my legs, arms and back, with their weather-beaten and notched batons.

From behind the bars at the police station, I saw my normally arrogant employer stand aside apologetically while Sunny's vulgar father spat expletives in the officer in-charge's face. In a couple of hours, the sly Doctor had stopped pushing his luck and was offering the OC bits of *paan masala* with pinches of *zarda*, while conniving to cook up a charge and have me dealt with severely. I was in pain and coughing up clots of dark blood.

Laboni and her tubercular husband wanted me to see a chest specialist they knew. But I needed to go home, forever. Return to the scented breeze in forests of pine, to the chatter of brooks through banks of maidenhair, to the bark of deer at dusk and to the choking call of invisible Ghural from shining rock precipices at dawn, that frightened broods of Khalij and Koklas pheasants who floated on soft clouds and glided, chuckling into forests of moist oak. I needed to go home; to the warmth of simple and caring kith and kin; to my wife, Anandi, whom I had ignored and neglected for almost thirty years. She had silently grown older, wrinkled and weak, without me. Alone, through repeated dry summers that led to meagre harvests. Alone, through frosty winters when most villages were deserted by all, except those who didn't have the strength to leave, or a place to go to. But she had never complained. Not even when Bheem, our only son, died. Our twenty-three-year-old son, who had never recovered from a depression after he had witnessed my mother fall off a cliff, while cutting grass for our buffaloes. He was born simple; Dr Fleming at the Mission Hospital had told us, he would stay like that all his life. He had thrown himself off the cliff where he had seen his grandmother fall. I hadn't come home then. From an STD booth in Landour, Anandi's nephew had begged me to return for a few days, to participate in the rituals they observed in the village for thirteen days.

The Mehras were having a party for over a hundred people, to celebrate their silver wedding anniversary and I realised how lost they would be without me. They gave me one thousand and one rupees as a tip. It cost seventy rupees at the post office to send the cash by money order to Anandi, for Bheem's *sraadh*. Nine hundred and thirty one wasn't a lot. I didn't hear from her. Like a fool, I never realised that almost all the money I sent Anandi every month, went towards paying off the loan I had taken from Uday's older brother six years ago, when my father had died.

Anandi sent me a bagful of juicy *kaaphals* last year, through a neighbour's son, who worked for a rich contractor in Gurgaon. She had gathered them from the forests on her way to the slopes above our village where she cut grass for a neighbour's cows. For her labours, they fed her a meal every day she worked. It usually consisted of *rotis* and *thechwaani*, a tasty dish of crushed *moolis* and crushed unpeeled potatoes, which I missed. Through every monsoon and autumn, till all the grass dried, died and disappeared for the year, Anandi never went to bed hungry. I had no idea, she had borrowed more money from Uday to pay for Bheem's funeral in Haridwar and for the *sraadh,* where she fed everyone in the village, as is our custom.

As I lay back on my bunk, an American missionary boarded the train. I knew one when I saw one. They all smelled of newsprint and scented wet wipes that disguised their unbathed and dry cleaned western filthiness. Mr Billington, with a boy aged about two strapped to his chest, held two girls aged between four and six by their wrists, one in each hand, and swung them on board. His pregnant wife sweated as she lifted strollers and bags of diapers and provisions. Tightfisted missionaries, even the Indian ones, simply never, ever, use coolies.

Unable to look at the poor pregnant woman struggle with a hefty suitcase that scraped along the passage on one wheel, I went up and helped her. Ruth memsahib had obviously never left a farm in America and now, as she explained to me much later, had come to India only 'because Nathan had been asked by Jesus to save Hindus and Sikhs'.

The exertion was more than I was ready for. I doubled over coughing and turned breathless. I had been let out of prison less than twenty-four hours ago and my insides still hurt very badly. I fell back against my bunk and saw the memsahib staring at me with deep concern. She seemed a kind person. I wiped the edge of my mouth and realised, I was still coughing up blood. Grabbing some paper napkins that were wrapped over their snacks, the memsahib innocently offered to help. Her husband cringed and asked her not to interfere. I had learned a long time ago, that foreigners offered help when it suited them. Expecting it, requesting it or ever taking it for granted, was an inexcusable native presumption. Oriental stupidity.

This wonderful night train to Dehra Dun was really a journey from earth to heaven. It was a slow, noisy and bumpy ride that made hundreds of stops through the night, at stations in jungles where herds of wild elephants roamed, where thugs boarded, craftsmen loaded shipments, saadhus mingled with *bahurupias* to preach or dupe pilgrims to the kingdom of the gods and army personnel alighted in hide-aways where camouflaged artillery, tanks and field guns poked dangerous heads, out of the tall elephant grass that lined both sides of the railway track.

Nathan gathered his family around him on the bunk and I could tell, he had begun to open the food they had brought on. A packet of chips was passed from hand to hand, followed by some kind of meat sandwiches and a bottle of mineral water.

Ruth looked at me and smiled as she chewed on the sandwich. The two girls looked over their Daddy's shoulder at me. The older one grimaced derisively, turned away and disappeared out of sight. The younger one, Alice, with sparkling blue eyes, stared at me as I opened my tiffen box. Inside were four *rotis*, some *bhindi sabzi* and two *laddoo*. I tilted the box in her direction, so she could get a good look at it all. Nathan looked around to see what was so interesting and immediately pulled his younger girl away. They had been taught, it was rude to stare. In truth, they were being taught, never to care.

Inside the rotis, I discovered a small piece of fish, cooked in pungent bengali mustard oil, that Laboni knew I loved. With all her problems, she was still such a caring and loving human being. Pinky would be happy with her. That made me happy, too. Alice was staring at me again from under her father's arm. I gestured to her to come close and tempted her with a *laddoo*. Quietly, she edged forward, slowly took the sweet from my hand and copying the way I bit mine, gingerly bit into her *laddoo*. As she popped in the crumbling *bundis* that were falling from the corners of her mouth, she smiled shyly and I burst out laughing. The father, Nathan, swung around and as soon as he realised what was going on, he grabbed the *laddoo* from Alice's hand and returned it to me. He then shook her and asked her to stand straight and thank the old man. She did. I smiled and reached out to touch her chin and give her a flying kiss. By then, she had been whisked away and placed on the far side of the bunk, beside her mother, from where we couldn't see one another. As I put away my tiffen box and prepared to go to sleep, I saw Ruth break a bar of chocolate into four and divide it amongst them.

Early in the morning, as the train pulled into Haridwar, I got off to get some tea. It was the best tea you could drink anywhere, in any railway station in India and served in clean cups with a saucer, just like the sahibs drank it. In the east, through the twisted railings and above the smoke rising out of a distant colony, a blazing red sun was rising gloriously. Monkeys were already prancing along the roof of the train, hoping to snatch anything from bananas to garlands of marigold from unwary sleepy pilgrims who got off by the hundreds here, to bathe in the Ganga.

Haridwar was where an engine was added on to help the train climb into the Shivaliks. I had just sipped my tea when I saw Ruth trying to step down at the exact same time as the new engine came into position and hit the last bogie. Ruth was about to fall. I threw my cup down and ran across the platform to grab her before she fell. Nathan, who had seen it all happen from inside, came running to the compartment door and looked angrily at his pregnant wife as if she were to blame for what had happened. To cheer them up, I told them about the excellent tea and offered them some. Nathan took Ruth by the elbow and helped her back on board. Ruth turned at the door and thanked me for saving her and then they disappeared into the darkness of the train.

I went to my berth and pulled out my wallet from my bag. I counted out ten rupees, which is how much the vendor wanted for the cup I had broken. As I walked back out, I saw Nathan looking very disapprovingly at me. He obviously didn't like my touching his wife. There was nothing I could have done to avoid it. She could have hurt herself badly. The train began to pull out. I was beginning to feel a stabbing pain in my side. By the time I had paid for the tea and jumped back on, I was dizzy. I stuck my head out of the door and got sick just as the train entered a tunnel. When we emerged, I caught a fleeting glimpse of the Ganga and the sun-kissed mountains beyond.

I walked slowly back to my seat and lay down. Ruth looked concerned and whispered something to Nathan. They all turned to look at me and then silently looked away. The train rattled on; over parched riverbeds and through forests where black racquet-tailed drongos and white paradise flycatchers were swooping around rain trees, gulmohars and jacarandas. I can remember the sight of blossoms on mango trees. Then, very gently, all my pains began to subside and disappeared. The perfume of ripe mangos, *litchis*, roses, gardenias came to me in wonder filled wafts and then the mystical scent of lantanas filled the air.

When the train came to a halt in Dehra Dun, Nathan hurried his children past me. Ruth stopped, looked at me, sent the girls ahead with their dolls and whispered to Nathan. He nodded and lifted my arm over my chest and then noticed my open wallet lying on the floor. As he picked it up, there was shouting and someone ordering people to quickly get out of the compartment. Four sturdy policemen, fattened on junk food sold on railway platforms, shoved everyone aside and stood looking at me as if I was about to devour them. Then, one of them pulled my bag from under my head and began rummaging inside it and another tentatively felt inside my pockets and emptied their contents. Ruth had joined the girls. Nathan looked contemptuously at what was happening and walked away.

Uday had just climbed almost two thousand feet from our village with twenty litres of milk in cans tied on his back. The forests of rhododendron trees were aflame with blossoms and the paths beneath the trees were carpeted in red. Long-tailed red-billed magpies hovered like sunbirds drinking dew and nectar from the flowers and tourists flocked to take pictures of the roads and trees. Uday hardly noticed them. He came to sell his milk, seven days a week, year in year out. As he sat at the little tea-stall down the road beside St Paul's church and smoked a *biri*, he knew his hip and his knees wouldn't be able to take this for many more years. Far below, on the slopes above Kanda gaon, smoke was rising from a forest fire that had begun the previous day. From the looks of it, it was going to be yet another dry summer.

While Negi, the tea-stall owner, was pouring out his daily allotment of milk from the cans, he turned animatedly to Uday and asked him if he had met Ranbir and heard about Trilok in Delhi. Uday, of course, hadn't. When he was told of how his old friend had been caught stealing jewelry and had been put in prison, he turned pale. It couldn't be true. Never. Negi insisted it was. He said that he had heard it from the boy, Ranbir, who worked in Gurgaon, who last year had taken *kaaphals* from Anandi to Trilok. Ranbir had gone down to the village earlier in the morning. Uday hadn't seen him on the path. He was disturbed and hoped, Anandi wouldn't hear of all this. He told Negi that he would come back the next day with a phone number in Delhi that Negi could call to ascertain the truth about this terrible story.

Back in Dehra Dun, they had tied my feet and hands with ropes and put me on a luggage trolley. It was pushed to the end of the platform, out of sight. Twittering swallows in the sky meant summer was approaching. I had watched Uday climb up to Lal Tibba in Landour with his load of milk. His clothes were stained with weeks of sweat that left contours of rippled salt on his collar, his back and his arms. He wheezed as he neared the top. I thought of the days when we walked together on the hillsides and picked up rhododendrons from the ground to suck out their nectar and chew on the petals. They quenched our thirst. He would have been pleased to know I was coming back.

Police Inspector Kala had been summoned to the railway station. He looked at me and studied the contents of my pockets. The two constables who had been sitting with me and chatting about how Dehra Dun was changing for the worse, ever since it had become the capital of Uttarakhand, explained to Kala that I had no ID. They examined the signature bruises of a police thrashing on my neck, my back, my arms and legs and were worried that they would be held responsible for it. On a lovely spring morning, no one was interested in inviting trouble and complicating the lives of an overworked and underpaid police force's uncomplicated existence. The dried blood around my mouth had flies sitting on it. Kala chased them away with a swish of his baton. I almost blinked. With no claimants and no form of identification to trace the origin or destination of a person, it was always best to leave the dirty work to the city's municipal sweepers who knew their job and performed it skilfully.

Nathan was an honest Christian. When he got home, he looked inside my wallet and found two thousand and seven hundred rupees in it. St Pauls church, in Landour, had just constructed a commemorative monument in stone with a slate plaque on it, on the grass near its front gate. With the chaplain still not back from his Easter break, the secretary of the community had a problem gathering the funds needed to pay the chaps who built it. The cost was only two thousand and five hundred rupees because the stones used had come from the hillside behind the church, just as the rocks had once to build the church a century ago. Nathan gave the church the money. The church was very grateful and thanked the Billingtons at the next Sunday service. Unfortunately, try as much as she did, Ruth was unable to persuade the church's committee to put Trilok's name down in its records, as a donor. It was clear that donations from pagan heathens while welcomed in practice, couldn't be acknowledged in principle, particularly when associated with paying for a monument like the one in question.

What had begun as an ordinary brush fire had now become a raging forest fire and one could hear its crackle and see fireballs of resin fly across the sky, from the plush living rooms of gentry who lived in romantic cottages on the slopes of Landour.

That evening, when Uday got back to his village, he dumped the provisions he had bought in Mussoorie at home and rushed to Anandi's house to tell her that the rumours of Trilok stealing and being put in jail were absolutely false and that Trilok had left Delhi permanently and would be home any day now. Neighbours told Uday that they had seen Anandi climb up the hillside in the morning, as usual, to go and cut grass.

Uday found Anandi's sickle near the cowshed, covered in ash that had been carried by the wind and scattered over all the homes in Kanda.

For two hundred rupees, Nathan had bought four bars of chocolate from the tea-stall outside the church. Each member of the family was given one as they strolled happily down the road to their cottage overlooking the Doon Valley. Ruth may still weep in Nathan's alien fields but Alice, I knew, would discover her wonderland in India. My plastic wallet, empty but for a photograph of Anandi and me, taken when our son was born, was lying in a dustbin marked for recycling.

It was dusk. A lonely deer barked in the woods and an insomniac pygmy owlet began its plaintive hoot. The moon was rising over the snows of Gangotri. Like always, the world slowly and quietly went to sleep. Anandi and I were united, in peace, at last.

# Mussoorie House Names

Bill Aitken

The names given by Mussoorie's first British settlers to their bungalows reveal insights into the Raj and help explain why its rule barely lasted in the town for one hundred and thirty years. Hill-stations were created as summer retreats from the enervating heat. Not only individual officers escaped to the cooler mountain heights, but the whole apparatus of government in certain places shifted bag and baggage, to provide evidence (if any, were needed) that the British presence in India was doomed by the climate, to be short term. The British in India were essentially birds passage because of their unwillingness to adapt to the Indian topography and their insular reluctance to absorb, or be absorbed by Indian culture. Instead, like many Indian settlers abroad today, they withdrew within their own communities. In winter, they lived in their 'civil lines' and in summer, moved to their hill-stations to manage the affairs of the

East India Company, aloof from the heat, dust and *janata* of the pains. However, the stations they started from scratch have survived the departure of the Raj and maintained their unique identity with inputs both from Anglo–Saxon and Pahari culture.

Inevitably, nostalgia played a leading role in the naming of their bungalows and British names of places were translocated to the hills of Garhwal, to make the surroundings seem more like home. For example, the first resident of Mussoorie was Captain Young, an Irishman and his house at 'Mullingar' like others to come up in Landour (e.g. 'Trim Lodge', 'Shamrock Cottage') are named after places or things in Ireland, with which the captain had sentimental attachments. Scottish names abound more than English and this may be the fallout of the Biblical law of primogeniture in the former country which made it incumbent on younger sons to find their fortunes overseas. The absence of specific English names of places is surprising and it seems, the English preferred to name their bungalows after sylvan species: there are any amount of houses named after pines, firs, oaks, willows, maple and hazel.

In the 1968 Survey guidemap of Mussoorie and Landour (priced at two rupees and twenty-five paise), nine properties are listed with oak in their names and they run all the way from 'Oakgrove' (the first building on the climb from Rajpur by the original bridle path) to 'Oakville' the eastern-most house on Landour ridge. 'Oakgrove' campus is the school for railway officers' children, while 'Oakville' is the home of the talented Alter family. 'Seven Oaks' (now, demolished to provide staff quarters for Wynberg Allen School) situated at the bottom of Palpitation Hill was the estate of the *shikari*, Colonel Alfred Powell, while 'Four Oaks' at the top of the hill belonged to the Nabha royal family. Halfway up the hill, standing between these two sprawling bungalows is the appropriately named 'Acorns Cottage' with its original steep tin roof intact.

In the early 1830s, subscriptions were raised to build Christchurch at the centre of the town belonging to the Anglican (Church of England) dispensation. At the town's extremes were founded the two oldest religiously endowed schools, both still going strong and much sought after for their quality education. Waverley Convent follows the Roman Catholic ritual and Woodstock School at the other end of the theological spectrum, supports the Presbyterian faith. A third college, St George's in Barlowganj, continues as a premier Catholic institution because of the dedication of the Irish Brothers, who were indifferent to the fate of the Raj. What is intriguing about the disparate beliefs of 'Waverley' and 'Woodstock', is their both choosing names directly from the works of Sir Walter Scott. At least, a dozen houses in Mussoorie (and especially Landour) continue to boast names from Scott's literary canon, an extraordinary compliment to that Scottish writer's genius and a comment on the Victorian taste for British history, enlivened with romance and adventure.

However, in real life, a romantic adventurer like 'Raja' Wilson of Harsil who owned at least two properties in Mussoorie named after Scott's fiction—'Ivanhoe' and 'Rokeby'—was kept at arm's length from polite society. Wilson who made a fortune floating deodar logs down the Bhagirathi from Harsil, married a local lass and to make matters worse, she was the daughter of a temple drummer from Mukhba. However, this humbly born hill woman possessed the character to manage her affairs so well, that she was entrusted with playing hostess in Rajpur to Lady Dufferin, the most snobbish of all the vicereiness. It is interesting to note that today's State Bank of India building in Kwality Chowk is listed by the 1968 Survey map under its old name and designation as the 'Himalayan Bank' of which Raja Wilson was a director. There are over three hundred and thirty named properties listed on the modern survey map. Some of their oblong cast-iron nameplates which were bolted into the gate pillars still exist.

Another *Angrez* sahib who married a local lady was one of the settlement's earliest administrators. The building of his house 'Cloud End' at the western-most point of Mussoorie was supervised by the travel writer, Fanny Parkes. Her neighbour in the 1830s was Col George Everest, whose 'Park Estate' was home to the greatest land survey ever made on our planet, and which earned his name its place on top of the world's highest mountain. If nostalgia determined the earliest house names, money and clout were harnessed to increase the later demand for prestige from royals (like 'Kapurthala Chateau'), or industrialists ('Birla House' in Happy Valley), who hoped to leave their mark on Mussoorie. (The exiled Dalai Lama would stay at 'Birla House' before settling in Dharamshala.)

Hill village economy never allowed for the accumulation of capital, so the hillman was constrained to fill in vacancies as hotel bearer for rich hoteliers from the plains. After Independence, lawyers and retired government servants were also able to acquire houses to announce a shift from the landed to the middle classes. Accordingly, the changed house names reflect the bland mainstream choices, consistent with horizons unfamiliar with the town's British connexions. In more recent years, popular saints and television *mahatmas* have acquired properties for their summer residence, and obviously, their houses reflect the names dear to their familiar sect, but own little relevance to the essential character of Mussoorie.

Some may detect a triumphalist choice in names like 'Sebastopol', 'St Helens' and 'Palmerston'. Certainly, the idea of paramountcy was upper-most in the minds of the civic fathers who framed Mussoorie's bye-laws. Hand-in-hand with the wish to maintain a cultural haven exclusively for Whites was the conscious distancing of the locals and their places of worship. One reason for the well-preserved status of the hill-station's old properties was a municipal tax concession for those who kept their tin roofs painted. The earliest bungalows can still be detected by steep slope of their tall tin roofs. This style may have been borrowed from the original *shikari's* huts which copied the Gujjar mode of thatching.

Large properties would have a main house with a cottage named after it. Every house and cottage has a history to tell and sometimes, a ghost to reckon with. Ruskin Bond has described how Miss Bean was forced after Independence, to mortgage her Arundel property to a local *lala*. The main house passed on to a lawyer who entered judicial folklore by seeking to prosecute Mrs Indira Gandhi for allegedly stealing a chicken during the Emergency. The cottage was bought by a maharaja to house his servants and one of these surreptitiously sold half of the maharaja's land. With the ill-gotten gains, the servant built a poultry farm but met with an untimely end, when he was crushed by the vehicle he had bought to market his eggs. In recent years, the cottage was demolished for a resort hotel.

It might be noted, the British accepted the local names for natural features such as Rispana *nadi,* Khattapani *khal* and Pari *tibba*. Today, Landour is noted for its Defence Institute but formerly, the whole hillside in the summer was the seat of foreign missionaries gathered to attend the Language School, where the entire gamut of North Indian languages were taught on a most scientific basis at Kellogg Church. Landour Cantonment Depot once had both Catholic and Protestant

churches to suggest that Irish Catholic regiments were once billeted in the barracks. 'Seaforth Lodge' echoes the posting of a Protestant highland regiment.

Some caution has to be exercised in interpreting the evidence of house names in Mussoorie, since all the several layers of settlers have been more concerned to create impressions that further historical accuracy. The town's name itself, believed by the British to derive from a local plant (masur), seems too neat a theory and may have been invented to throw people off the scent. The fact is, all the locals pronounce the name of the town as 'Mansuri' not 'Masuri'. Why should Garhwalis corrupt their own usage? Mansur was said to be a dacoit who had his base in these hills and it would not do to have a hill station named after a bandit. The John Company forces had a hard time pacifying the Doon area and readers of Jim Corbett will recall that the dacoit Sultana stalked the neighbouring hills well into the twentieth century. Curiously, modern tourist couples to Mussoorie have their photographs taken as a memento of the town, with the lady wearing hill dress and the man dressed as bandit, complete with the villain's eye patch!

Names like 'Kincraig' that began as a Scottish (Gaelic) import has, over the years, been transformed by local usage to 'King Krek' and I have heard Dotials pronounce it at 'Concrete'! 'The Library' has escaped mutilation by translation to become 'Kitab Ghar' and 'Waverley' likewise, escapes mauling by the descriptive 'Kala Pushta' (the wall of the black nuns). That quintessential Raj avenue 'The Mall' has overcome time and prejudice to maintain its status as a place to strut and 'Camel's Back' has also survived in the original. Not so fortunate was the rambling hilltop estate above St Mary's hospital, once known as 'Evelyn Hall' and which has all the elegant trappings of what looks like the town's former Church of Scotland. Now badly run down, it goes by the name of 'Sahu Jain Estate'.

Christchurch, the town's most impressive ecclesiastical edifice, survives as the official church of the Raj, but its shrunken congregation has a hard time maintaining its earlier style. Fortunately, its architecture like that of St Paul's in Landour is attractive and stout enough to attract restoration funds from outsiders. By contrast, the Methodist Church in Kulri and the Union (Baptist) Chapel nearby, being less dependent on British officialdom and more attuned to Indian rites of worship, have thriving congregations along with services in the vernacular.

To show how important it is to keep an open mind on the twists and turns that popular history can take, till quite recently it was widely believed that Maharaja Dilip Singh, heir to the emperor, Ranjit Singh of the Punjab, was interred by the British in 'Castel Hill Estate', presently occupied by the Survey of India in Landour bazaar. However, the British guardian of the Sikh prince has written a journal of his Mussoorie stay and the castle the prince stayed in was actually 'Whyt Bank Castle', the residence till recent years of St George's College staff. This famous building, linked by a suspension bridge to the college campus, has now been transformed into the *JP Manor Residency Hotel.* It is true that Dilip Singh was the technical owner of the Kohinoor diamond, now part of the British crown jewels. However, he never enjoyed physical possession of the stone and was coached by his British mentors, to formally present it to Queen Victoria.

Another political detainee was an Emir of Afghanistan whose bungalow came to be called 'Bala Hissar' after the fort in Kabul. Today, the site is part of Wynberg Allen School and known as the 'Bahunguna Science Block' after the famous mountaineer, who was an old boy of the school and died tragically on an international Everest expedition.

Unlike Simla and Nainital which were the official summer seats of government, as a non-official hill station, Mussoorie attracted the pleasure-loving more than the strait-laced. 'Hakman's' and 'Stiffles' night clubs were once patronised by a bevy of royal residents who proved such princely spenders that by the 1930s cabaret acts from London and Paris were the norm. This roisterous lifestyle had begun almost a century earlier and the 'Himalaya Club' (still running as a motel) finds mention for its riotous activities (including dueling to the death) in Charles Dickens' magazine *Household Words*. Mussoorie formerly boasted two breweries that harnessed the natural springs at 'McKinnon's' (now, DLF) and 'Whymper's Pool' (near Colonel Skinner's 'Sikander Hall'). The advent of the cinema saw Mussoorie boast four halls with three shows a day. In the heyday of Hollywood, the royals who had their own boxes would watch all three shows at the 'Majestic', 'Picture Palace' and later, the 'Rialto'.

Mussoorie remains remarkable for its cosmopolitan flavour and the enviable standard of education provided by its schools. Mention must be made of the Anglo-Indian contribution to the sound educational standards. The Doon's distinction as a centre of learning excellence, derives from the dedication and professionalism of the Anglo-Indian teachers. One of the last of the great school-marm's is Miss Edith Garlah nearing a hundred years in age whose 'Woodlands Estate' in Landour was formerly a private school.

When I first visited Mussoorie in 1960, I stayed at 'Wolfsburn', a delightful guest house in upper Landour run by an Anglo-Indian lady, Mrs Walsh for students learning Hindi. A dozen years later, when I decided to settle in Mussoorie, I was sad to hear Mrs Walsh had passed away and her house sold to a contractor. The latter, unmindful of the elegance and antiquity of this bungalow, demolished it in the mistaken belief that the 'memsahib' was as foolish as he was, and had hidden away treasure in its walls.

Mussoorie's future as a tourist destination will be the preservation, rather than the destruction of the quality artifacts of the Raj era. Landour Bazaar, for example, has an ambience, unique amongst hill-stations. The town's earliest-named buildings, 'Mullingar', 'Zephyr Lodge', 'Companybagh' and 'Cloud End', are still in use and have become a part of Mussoorie folklore. Each has a rich history that taken together, contribute to the hill-station's mystique as a special destination in modern 'Dev Bhumi'. Even the *kawarias,* on their pilgrimage to fetch *Ganga jal* from *Har ki Pauri,* now include Mussoorie *darshan* as part of their itinerary.

# Milk Rusk to Maharaja Mac

Palash Krishna Mehrotra

Six years ago, I moved to Dehra Dun. It is a pleasant hill town full of retired folk, boarding schools and bakeries selling plum cakes, sausages, milk biscuits and stick-jaws. It is also an unpleasant place, marked by fumy traffic jams, sleepy multi-cuisine restaurants where politicians in white kurta-pyjama drink Mona Lisa beer, and wannabe lounge bars which routinely erupt in stag violence.

Being a man of contradictions, I liked this combination of purity and pollution, of north-Indian sleaze and colonial gentility. At the time I was in my mid-20s, I wanted to write books, tell stories but didn't know where to start, where to go. I wanted to be left alone to find my feet. But too much isolation frightened me. I wanted to be able to walk out into a market or a busy thoroughfare, when the reading got too hot to handle. I wanted to be close enough to the mountains so that on a clear day, after a night of rain, I could stretch my hands and touch them. I wanted to be able to drive out into the city and get stuck in a poisonous jam where the mind, along with the traffic, comes to an absolute standstill. Rajpur Road, with the clocktower at one end and Rajpur village at the other, both afforded me pleasures.

I began frequenting a bakery in the heart of the town. I would go almost every other day to have a lemon tart and a cup of coffee. Meanwhile, things were changing. Old shops disappeared overnight; new ones took their place almost immediately. Dusty, opaque fronts made way for snazzy, glass-fronted showrooms. Pizza parlours, burger joints, coffee bars and big music stores opened on the high street. The owner of the bakery, finding it hard to survive in the new environment, quietly moved out one weekend. For a couple of weeks there was no activity. The shop remained boarded up; a beggar took up position in front of the downed shutters. Then, the workers arrived. They pulled the bakery down and installed the gleaming, new outlet of a fast-food chain in its place. Not being much of a sentimentalist, I went along one day to have a look. I ordered a meal and was waiting for the cashier to return my change, when I overheard the waiters trading a joke about Guy Ritchie and Madonna. I was amazed because the conversation was taking place in English.

When I went to Barista, the man who made my latte spoke to me about the weather in English. In Planet M, the salesgirl wanted to know why I bought so many Woody Allen films. And, once in the Polo Bar, I was joined at my perch by three coffee-shop workers on their day off. We drank fancy cocktails. Spoke about Justin Timberlake and *Rang de Basanti*. All in English.

It struck me, for the first time, that these western-style outlets have done more than add a dash of neon to an already colourful Indian bazaar. The humble pizza has been the medium

for a genuine socio-cultural linguistic shift, creating a brand new class of people, in a country where speaking English once categorically demonstrated that you were above manual labour and above serving yourself, let alone others. They are India's first English-speaking 'working class,' an entirely new class adding another layer to an already complex society. They are willing to abandon desk jobs—almost a birthright for those who speak English—for physical work on the shop floor.

For generations, English-speaking Indian kids were forced into a handful of professions by their parents, aptitude notwithstanding. An Indian father would sit his adolescent son down and lay out the options: medicine, engineering, banking, government jobs. Middle-class Indians had historically displayed an aversion to manual work. If you were educated and English-speaking, you did not lift a finger. The driver washed your car on Sundays and you never even made yourself a cup of tea—the maidservant was there to do that. If your father worked in a bank, you would not dream of taking a job in a restaurant kitchen. In the Indian context, you belonged to the middle class, not the working class.

The average Indian's attitude to work has changed. While a section of the young in the Islamic world seethes with resentment, young Indians are in love with the American lesson that education, competition and hard work bring prosperity. Accompanying this feeling is a new-found respect for physical labour. Class barriers, too, have broken down in these showrooms for global capitalism. The bank manager's son works side by side with a new migrant to the city and they both start with a clean slate. Caste identity usually resides in the surname, so when workers wear name tags bearing only their first names, centuries of prejudices are instantly wiped out.

Rajpur Road is where the action is. The big chains are all there: Planet M, Music World, Dominos, Pizza Hut, Nirula's, Barista and Café Coffee Day. It acts as a honey pot for young men and women from the neighbouring hills, who want to become part of the new economy. At the same time, the hospitality industry has given people wings. There are young men and women coming in from other states. They bring with them a sense of possibility—both physical and mental. These new immigrants represent the throbbing world that lies beyond the mountains, a new economy which has turned a country of gated private parks, into a giant playground open to all.

Ram Chandra Singh, a carpenter's son, is twenty-five. He comes from Nagrajdhar, a remote village in the western Himalayas. For his college education he came to Mussoorie, a hill station dubbed 'Queen of the Hills' by the British. While pursuing his B.A., he took a part-time job working at Club Mahindra, a time-share resort. The move from village to city wasn't easy, but the Pizza Hut on Rajpur Road made it easier. 'Of course, one feels awkward in the beginning. But I like it here. There is no hierarchy. On busy days, even the manager rolls up his sleeves and does the dishes. I am allowed to take my own decisions.' Ram acquired basic skills in English from a small hole-in-the-wall institute, one of the many that have mushroomed in post-liberalisation Dehra Dun. The Finesse, for example, offers 'Special courses for Housewives, students, aspirants and professionals.' Rosemount's promises to make English 'easier than your mother tongue.' Or, you can go to Mentor—its catch line, following Protagoras, is 'Mentor is the measure of all things.' While the quality of instruction is often not very high, these private institutes serve their function: equipping their students with a functional knowledge of English, that enables them to join the global workforce, even if at the lowest level. Nehru once said that 'English would be more widely known in India in the future than now; though it will not be known for better quality.' His prophecy has come true. It is the diploma in English that puts a spring in Ram's step, gives him the confidence to walk around Pizza Hut, like he owns the place. It allows him to penetrate an alien neon world, one which must have seemed impossibly foreign and forbidding from the outside.

Chirag's father is a senior manager with a bank. Like Ram, he works in Pizza Hut and has no qualms about it. 'Look at that,' he says pointing at a poster hanging on the wall. It advertises 'cool jobs' for people with 'passion, dedication, mania.' Next to it is another poster. It shows Olympic rings filled with pizza topping. Chirag is the 'achiever of the month.' His face has been given pride of place behind the cashier's desk. He is 'Lord of the Rings.' 'Initially,' he says in a quiet voice, 'my father had a problem. He said it's not a good career, serving at tables. Now, he understands that this is not the same as working for another restaurant. This is a multinational, so there is glamour attached to it. I don't think sweating it out to earn a living is such a demeaning thing. The Indian fast-food industry is growing at forty per cent per annum. There are avenues for growth. If I am good at my work, then in a few months, I can rise to a higher position.'

Both these stories are revealing in their own ways. In a developing economy like India's, unlike in the West, McJobs are not seen as soul-killing. The bank manager's son is happy to be seen doing manual labour—something he wouldn't have agreed to, ten years ago—because there is 'glamour' to those corporations, no matter what the work. For the carpenter's son, a vernie (vernacular) boy from a remote Himalayan village, it gives him a foothold in the city. It provides him with an entry into the world of modern jobs. He teaches himself the ways of the world, by observing his customers and watching training videos supplied by his employers.

McJobs have also encouraged people to move around, to leave the streets they were born in—traditionally, from childhood to marriage and death, a lot of Indians never do—and explore their huge country. The lucky few even get to see a bit of the world beyond. Amit works at the Yo! China, opposite St Joseph's school. Five years in a youthful fast-food industry, and the man is a veteran. He comes from Garhmukteshwar, a village near Meerut, around forty miles from Delhi. His village has no electricity. His uncle and aunt are illiterate. They cannot fathom what he does. He is a little embarrassed about his uncle and aunt and refuses to discuss them. He did a course in hotel management, straight after school. He has worked for Café Coffee Day, Barista, Costa Coffee and Pizza Hut. He has seen a fair bit of the country—Delhi, Chandigarh, Pune, Bangalore—which is something his parents and relatives could only dream of, and has just returned from a training stint in Thailand. At twenty-three, he has a team working under him. He writes poetry in Hindi. He picked up basic English at an institute in Dehra Dun. The rest, he picked up on the job. 'Globalisation has been kind to me,' he says. 'One has to change oneself. Sometimes, it is necessary to break with tradition.' He acknowledges the power of travel. 'You go down south, and it's a different world. In Bangalore, engineers walk in for a cappuccino and all the conversation is about making jet engines quieter and turbines more efficient. I met a guy who works for Motorola, writes software for new phones; there was someone from Intel—his team was doing things like fine-tuning wireless broadband technology. I wouldn't have met these people in Garhmukteshwar. I like meeting new people. When I meet them, I also learn. Maybe, my kids will end up working for these IT majors, one day.'

For others, these new restaurants and shops have enabled them to discover their hidden talents. Gaurav Joshi is a lean, wiry twenty-three-year-old who left his village three years ago and hasn't gone back since. He stays in regular touch with his family on his mobile phone. 'My father wanted me to join government service. He kept harping on about job security. But, that is the old way of thinking. Now, you can start young and work at various things, find out what you're good at. Job security is not that important.' He works as a chef at Mark Pi's Crazy Noodles, an American chain specialising in Chinese food and designer wobbly tumblers for beverages. Joshi discovered his passion for cooking as a schoolboy. 'There was an emergency in the family. My mother had to leave suddenly. We were totally helpless without her. I tried to make *rotis*; they got burnt. Everything I tried to cook, got burnt. But I liked being in the kitchen—the heat of the fire, the smell of spices roasting in oil. When my mother came back, I started spending more and more time in the kitchen.'

Before, his chosen career would hardly have been seen as cool. Now, it is. 'I am not seen as a workhorse cook working in some drab kitchen. I am a chef in a crisp white hat. We have an open kitchen, so the customers can see me work. They get very impressed when the flames leap past my ears. Especially, the ladies. Just the other day, this really smart girl came up to me and asked me out to coffee. Imagine, this happening ten years ago—an English-speaking, middle-class Indian girl wanting to go out with a cook. I said no. I already have a girlfriend.'

His kitchen-mate, Ashutosh, is from Delhi. He has also been cooking since he was a schoolboy. Being from Delhi, he has a larger range of references. He went to a good state school, so he speaks fluent English. He likes listening to Enrique Iglesias and Ricky Martin. He likes watching movies on HBO. He is happy to be independent. 'At home, you always have to change the channel when your father is around. He can't handle kissing scenes in Hollywood films, or my girlfriends calling. Here, I am on my own. Of course, there is a generational shift. I'll be less bothered if one day, my daughter has a boyfriend.'

It's not just the boys who see and exploit these new opportunities. In Yo! China, I meet a shy, pretty girl called Amandeep. Five years ago, no girl would be caught dead serving in a Dehra Dun restaurant. But these chains are different. They have a reputation for treating everyone equally. Parents do not have a problem letting their daughters work in these places, because they are safe, brightly lit, not sleazy. Amandeep says, her role model is her mother, a housewife. She is following a childhood dream—to become an air hostess and see the world. She goes to Frankfinn, an air-hostess training school just down the road from Yo! China. Her part-time job here helps pay for its expensive fees. Aruna, twenty-five, has been working at Café Coffee Day for the last two and a half years. She would not trade this for anything else. She wants to be named 'Brewmaster' of the northern region in the championships the company organises regularly. 'I work here ten hours a day and love every minute of it,' she says. 'Outside, you walk down the street and men stare at you, harass you. Inside, I am safe. It's like, I am not in Dehra Dun anymore.' Avantika is studying for a degree in commerce and has been able to move to a new city and start a new life because of her job. 'There were problems at home. Pizza Hut helped me to leave that behind. Now that I am earning, I can also help out my family rather than just sit around waiting to get married to some boy they choose for me. I have more respect now.'

All this independence at a young age, means that people are staying single for longer. This might not mean the complete dismantling of the arranged marriage system, but it does mean that people have relationships until the time they go in for a partner of their parents' choice. Long working hours in small spaces mean more workplace romances, some of which are converted into marriage, thus contributing to the breakdown of caste and class barriers. Pradeep is twenty-five and flips Maharaja Macs at the crowded McDonald's in Astley Hall. He dismisses marriage with a dramatic wave of the hand. 'Not till thirty-two. I have a girlfriend. On my day off, I like to take her for long drives on my Honda CBZ bike. Sometimes, we go half the way up to Mussoorie. The world is changing. You want to be part of this change, rather than getting tied down at an early age. The organisation shows us videos of westerners working in these joints in their countries. We see how they behave, boys and girls working as equals, being free with each other. We too want to be like them.' Amandeep's parents have also stopped pestering her to hurry. 'They know, my ambition is to take to the skies. They respect that. I will probably find a man in the same profession. But all that is for later. Right now, I have to focus on my job.'

Amandeep's boss, Amit, strikes a cautionary note. After five years in the business, he feels there is an urgent need to look beyond 'the glitz and the glamour,' the neon, the air-conditioning and the loud music. 'That's what attracts an eighteen-year-old, initially. Soon, he realises that the working hours are long. There is hardly any free time. Kids get frustrated. They come with unrealistic expectations. They want to buy the expensive Reebok sports jacket the customer is wearing, but cannot. Salaries are not that high.' He's also critical of the management. 'In the West, these things followed a more organic process. All we do is import, stick labels on things. Somebody buys a franchise—all he wants to do is make money from it, recover investment. They work you like a dog. In the West, people get breaks; there is more leisure time. You don't just go on and on and on, like here.' He mentions a friend in Delhi who committed suicide and another, who has picked up a drug habit along the way. 'It's not easy balancing work, family, girlfriend. Some people just crack up.'

Devinder Prajapati, a tall, gaunt-faced man of twenty-two, has a different take. He has been with McDonald's for three years. He comes from a small town in Punjab. I meet him on a Sunday. He is here even though it is his day off. He did a course in 'catering technology.' It taught him a bit of French but not much English. He shows me two books: *Developing Communication Skills* and *How to Write Correct English*. He shows me a page from the second book. The erroneous sentence appears on the left of the page; the correct version on the right ('The servant is attending on him / The servant is attending to him'). He says he picks up a lot, just by listening to his customers' conversations. He agrees that the work hours are long, but finds nothing wrong with it. 'Look, I don't want any free time. What would I do with it? When I am doing nothing, silly thoughts come into my head. They scare the shit out of me. Today is my day off, but I was going mental, sitting in my room. I thought, why not go back to McDonald's, hang out for a bit? On a weekday I would be in uniform—today I can wear civvies,' he says, casting a surreptitious glance at someone's gleaming Nike pumps.

Amit feels the kids are being slave-driven. Devinder, on the other hand, could hang around in his workplace, twenty-four hours a day. For him, this symbolises a move up from where he was. The fancy Japanese cars on Rajpur Road, the air-conditioned workspace, the throbbing music, the false politeness and the perfumed armpits not only seduce him, they make him feel good about himself; he does not want to be anywhere else. Make no mistake. He's lovin' it. But what about his children? Will they rise in *Fight Club*-style rebellion against soul-killing monotony? It is difficult to say. At the moment, Ram is thrilled to have a job—a regular job in a country of a billion people. He doesn't seem too bothered about his soul. Salvation was never on the menu.

# Nehru's Love Affair with Dehra Dun

Raj Kanwar

*Nehrus have had a life-long love affair with the twin towns of Dehra Dun and Mussoorie. The patriarch, Moti Lal would generally spend his summer vacations in Mussoorie. Jawahar Lal's first visit to Mussoorie was in the summer of 1906—as a sixteen-year-old. His last trip to Dehra Dun was on 23rd May 1964. On the evening of 26th May, Nehru flew back to Delhi. He was not destined to see the sunrise, the following day. He died in coma on the afternoon of 27th May.*

*It was the evening of Tuesday the 26th day of May 1964. The scene of action was the Cantonment Polo Grounds in Dehra Dun.*

Jawaharlal Nehru haltingly climbed the few steps of the helicopter stairway, his usual brisk gait missing. Indira followed him very close, as if she feared her Papu might stumble.

That was the end of his four-day visit to Dehra Dun for rest and recuperation after the stroke that he had suffered on 8 January, at the Bhubaneshwar AICC session. In the quiet environs of the Bhubaneshwar Raj Bhawan, where Nehru stayed, he slowly recovered. He remained in convalescence on his return to Delhi; his working hours substantially curtailed, even though the gravity of his illness was not publicly disclosed.

Here, let us digress a little in order to put Nehru's illness in proper political perspective. 'After Nehru, who?' question had assumed a shrill and repetitive stridency. Rumours were afloat that Indira would be inducted into her father's Cabinet with an important portfolio. The routine work of the Prime Minister was already being shared between Gulzari Lal Nanda and T.T. Krishnamachari. Later, Lal Bahadur Shastri was made a minister without portfolio; he was allocated much of the Prime Minister's responsibilities.

Public opinion surveys were then not much in vogue. However, Shastri, Kamaraj, Indira and Morarji Desai had won approval in that order, in a survey conducted by the Institute of Public Opinion.

Nehru had addressed a crowded press conference on 22 May, on the eve of his departure for Dehra Dun. When the question, 'After Nehru, who?' was repeatedly asked, Nehru felt annoyed at one stage, and stoutly retorted, 'My life is not ending so very soon'. In the midst of the applause that his retort evoked, no one then imagined, how false his declaration was going to turn. Alas, Nehru's life ended, within five days of that un-prophetic assertion.

Reverting to Dehra Dun, neither any one in the assembled farewell party at the helipad, nor among the large throngs that had earlier cheered Nehru and waved at him during his short drive from the Circuit House, could have dreamt that the sunset that evening would be his last, and that he would not see another sunrise.

Nehru stood at the open doorway of the helicopter, and looked back, almost blankly at the small and assorted farewell group. There were Congress leaders, senior civil and defence officers as per the protocol, and a few journalists, this writer included.

A pale, faint smile appeared on his otherwise rosy countenance. In retrospect, and ruminating over my impressions of that evening, I realised that his left hand was less active than his right. Nehru's left knee appeared somewhat stiff, hampering his brisk trademark gait. Those were, perhaps, the after-effects of the stroke that had afflicted him early that January. Nehru did not appear his usual cheerful self, though he tried hard to keep pretences, and succeeded, to some extent. He waved at us jauntily with his right hand, but that seemed a laboured effort. There was a strange sort of expression on his face. What did he wish to convey to those of us who had assembled there to bid him adieu? Was that to be the last and final good-bye? Did he have a premonition about his death? District Magistrate A.P. Dikshit, during whose tenure Nehru visited Dehra Dun on five occasions, had written a book on those visits in 1965 titled 'Antim Charan'. My impressions tallied with those of Dikshit.

On 25 May, Nehru talked many times of postponing his departure for Delhi by a day. He even indicated that he had some appointments in Delhi only on the afternoon of 27 May, and as such, he could easily leave for Delhi on 27th morning. So relaxed and comfortable he had felt in Dehra Dun that Nehru really yearned to extend his stay here. Dikshit cleverly noticed his desire and mustered courage to suggest extending his stay in Dehra Dun through May and June, adding that all important files and papers could be sent to Dehra Dun, '*aur saab, kaam yehan se ho jayega*'.

'*Haan, kaam to saab ho jayega*', Nehru replied philosophically. Was this a sort of fore-boding? But eventually, the scheduled departure on 26th afternoon was adhered to, since it was felt that it would give Nehru an overnight rest in Delhi, and enable him to attend to his appointments the following day, rested and refreshed.

But the hoped for overnight rest turned into a restless night. He awoke several times in the night, and was given a sedative by his trusted attendant, Nathu Ram. He awoke one final time before dawn. At about 6.30, Indira and physician, Bedi were summoned. Nehru seemed somewhat disoriented when the two appeared by his bedside, and asked 'What is the matter?' And then, he fell into a coma, and died at 1.44 p.m. on Wednesday, 27 May. Though he missed his scheduled appointments in Delhi that afternoon, he did keep the 'Final Appointment' with his Creator.

It was by sheer providence that Nehru had chosen to spend his last four days in Dehra Dun, the city he loved more than any other. Here, in the sylvan surroundings of the Circuit House under the shade of his favourite camphor tree, with birds as his companions, he felt at home, and at peace. He was far away from the maddening crowds of Delhi, the nagging question 'After Nehru, who?', and political intrigues. Here, he partook of simple vegetarian meals, took leisurely walks on the expansive lawns, sat under trees, and occasionally read.

He visited his old friend Sri Prakasa, former minister and governor, at Kotalgaon, eight miles uphill on the Mussoorie Road. He took lunch with his old colleague, and returned to the Circuit House late in the afternoon.

He and Indira also visited Sahastradhara late in the afternoon on the penultimate day of his stay in Dehra Dun. He was happy and pleased like a child who had just been given a chocolate bar. He and Indira enjoyed the view of the Sahastradhara sulphur springs, and the mountains beyond, sitting in the verandah of the PWD guest house, then just constructed. As the sun was setting far away in the horizon, Nehru returned to the Circuit House, feeling rejuvenated and relaxed with the excursion.

## *Nehru's Second Home*

Nehru had visited Dehra and Mussoorie on numerous occasions in the fifty-eight years, between his first visit in 1906 and the last on 23 May 1964. Many of those visits in the pre-1947 era were for rest and relaxation in the company of his father, mother, wife, daughter, sisters and nieces.

Even though Dehra Dun, in those pre-Independence years, was a small blip on India's political map, nonetheless, it attracted leaders of national eminence. In 1920, several senior leaders of the freedom movement such as Lala Lajpat Rai, Asif Ali, Saifuddin Kitchlu and Satyanand Stokes of Kotgarh, took part in a district political conference. Nehru too, participated in it.

Two years later, in July 1922, Nehru again addressed a political conclave at Doiwala—a sugarcane belt halfway between Dehra Dun and Rishikesh. That was followed by a provincial political conference in October, at which Moti Lal Nehru presided. The younger Nehru, again visited Dehra Dun in April 1924, and was presented a 'purse' of Rs 1900, a princely sum at that time, towards Tilak Swaraj Fund.

Political activity in Dehra Dun had gathered further momentum with announcement of elections to provincial legislative councils in the country. Moti Lal Nehru, Hakim Ajmal Khan, Maulana Abdul Kalam Azad, among others, addressed several election rallies in the district, and ensured the victory of the Congress candidate, Thakur Manjit Singh.

Other than the numerous visits that Nehru made willingly and happily, there were three involuntary visits when he was brought here as the 'guest' of the British government in India.

The first of such visits was in 1932, when Nehru and Govind Ballabh Pant were transferred to Dehra Dun from Bareilly jail. By January 1933, Nehru was all alone, his prisonmates were either released or transferred to other jails. For nearly eight months, Nehru virtually lived a solitary life. However, Nehru found solace in the company of the flowers that he had been allowed to receive from outside. He would daily do a bit of spinning. Nehru kept himself occupied in reading and writing. He wrote those famous letters to his daughter from the gaol.

The second of such visits was on 9 May 1934, on transfer from the Central Jail, Alipore, near Calcutta. He had been sentenced to undergo two years' simple imprisonment under section 124 of Indian Penal Code. He was hardly in Dehra Dun for three months, when he was again shifted, this time to Naini

Central Prison, near Allahabad. In prison terminology, a prisoner is not known by his given name, but is allocated a jail identity number. Nehru's was 95.

The next visit to Dehra Dun jail was on 9 November 1940, five days before his birthday. That time, he had been convicted under the draconian all embracing Defence of India Rules. His offence must have been serious enough to have compelled the judge to award him four years of rigorous imprisonment. But again, within a few months, on 28 February 1941 to be precise, Nehru was transferred to Lucknow's Central Prison. That time around Nehru's prison i.d. was 1948.

Dehra Dun jail then was quite small. Nehru was kept in an old lock-up which was outside the walled periphery of the prison but within its compound. The original jail building today stands on the left if one approaches the jail from Haridwar Road side. It is no longer a part of the present jail, but stands apart in decrepit isolation. The old lock-up has been converted into Nehru Block. The room, in which Nehru lived, is 8ft x 13ft with just one iron-barred window. Through this window, visitors would talk and interact with Nehru during his days of incarceration. Subsequently, for no rhyme or reason, the jail authorities raised the lower bricked part of the window to five feet and put a few more bars atop the narrow gaps. This stratagem deprived the visitor to have an eye contact with Nehru. Thus, the visitors could talk with Nehru, but could not see him, and vice versa. What a mean thing it was to do!

The room is sparsely furnished. The bed is a frame of iron rods, and criss-crossed iron strips provide the sleeping space. There is a straight chair with arms, and a small desk. The door opens into a small verandah with a toilet at the other end with an Indian style flush commode. Alongside is a tiny bathroom.

It was here in this cell, that Nehru began writing in June 1934, his much acclaimed Autobiography. The book was less than halfway through, when he was transferred to the Central Jail at Naini. It was completed in February 1935.

Though Nehru had experienced life in several jails in the then United Provinces and elsewhere, he always fancied Dehra Dun gaol.

I will let Nehru tell his reasons.

> *I had had better cells in other prisons but in Dehra Dun, I had one privilege which was very precious to me. The gaol proper was a very small one, and we were kept in an old lock-up outside the gaol walls, but within the gaol compound. The place was so small that there was no room to walk about it, and so were allowed, morning and evening, to go out and walk up and down outside the gate, a distance of about a hundred yards. We remained in the jail compound but this coming outside gave us a view of the mountains, and the fields, and public road...*
> *Only a prisoner...can appreciate the psychological value of these outside walks and open views. I loved those outings, and I did not give them up even during the monsoon when the rain came down for days in torrents, and I had to walk in ankle-deep water. I would have welcomed the outing in any place, but the sight of the towering Himalayas nearby was an added joy which went a long way in removing the weariness of the prison...when for many months, I was quite alone, I could gaze at these mountains I loved. I could not see the mountains from my cell, but my mind was full of*

*them, and I was ever conscious of their nearness, and a secret intimacy seemed to grow between us.*

[*An Autobiography*: JAWAHARLAL NEHRU]

Nehru also found Dehra Dun spring very pleasant, and far longer in duration than in the plains. Autumn too, was very pleasant. He also enjoyed winter, except when it rained.

*I remember one day in particular (24 December 1932). There was a thunderstorm and rain all day, and it was bitterly cold. Altogether it was one of the most miserable days . . . In the evening it cleared up suddenly, and all my misery departed when I saw all the neighbouring mountains and hills covered with a thick mantle of snow. The next day, Christmas day, was lovely and clear, with a splendid view of the snow-covered mountains.*

Nehru's love for the mountains remained till his very end.

### *Down memory lane with Nehru and Indira*

My acquaintance with Nehru–Gandhi family remained just that; mere acquaintanceship. Let me begin from the beginning. While still a student, I had become a stringer for four leading English daily newspapers in 1952–53. In the following year, I founded the *Vanguard* Weekly in partnership with Mr Jitender Nath who still owns it.

As a young journalist, my enthusiasm matched that of a new convert. Thus, the visits of Panditji and Indira Gandhi to Dehra Dun considerably whetted my journalistic appetite and

I often, found myself cycling to the Circuit House. Those visits, though, were not necessarily for news gathering but I did send brief stories about his arrival with a couple of quotes on how relaxed he felt. Nehru didn't believe in mixing business with holidays, and in fact, discouraged any official or political engagements. I don't remember having encountered any PAs or PSs accompanying Nehru on his visits to Dehra Dun; though there must have been one or two of his aides but they generally remained inconspicuous.

## *Meeting Nehru was a child's play*

Meeting Prime Minister Nehru was virtually child's play. No telephone calls, or prior appointments. In fact, there used to be only one telephone with a 3-digit number at the Circuit House and it used to be picked up either by its caretaker or the all-pervasive bearer, Ram Prashad who had become an animated fixture in the Circuit House.

One winter morning in mid-1950s, I cycled right up to the porch of the Circuit House and parked my bicycle against its outer wall. A couple of constables with *lathi*s stood at the main gate, a few lolled about in the front verandah, while some other sauntered inconspicuously deep on the big lawns under the shades of giant trees.

Unhurriedly, I approached Panditji who was strolling on the lawns and introduced myself as a stringer for *The Statesman* and the *Indian Express*. 'But I have no news to give'. Panditji said some words to that effect. 'Yes, I know. And, I have not come for news; I simply came to see you.' Panditji smiled. As I walked with him, I was tongue-tied. I couldn't find anything interesting or provocative for breaking the ice. As someone

more experienced, Panditji took the initiative to break the awkward silence and asked me what subjects did I study in the college. Then, in a rush of words, I briefly gave my academic background and further told him that I was the President of the DAV College Students' Union, two years before. That made him pause in his steps; he smiled again, and looked intently at me and then told me to come again if I wished. This implied invitation greatly encouraged and reassured me.

My sister, Neel Kamal, then worked as a welfare officer with the Indian Red Cross. She was a big fan of Pandit Nehru and Indira Gandhi. Unbeknown to me, she had knitted a woollen blouse for Indiraji and asked my advice on the best mode of its presentation. 19 November, was just a couple of days away and what better occasion could one find than Indiraji's birthday, for giving that unique present.

## *Rajiv and Sanjay*

Rajiv and Sanjay were then in The Doon School. On her visits to Dehra Dun, Indira Gandhi would often take the boys out if the school's rules permitted. Neither Pandit Nehru nor Indira Gandhi ever threw their weight about and behaved very deferentially with the then headmaster, John Martyn and K.C. Joshi, housemaster of Kashmir House, in which the two boys lived. Both Martyn and Joshi treated Nehru and Indira like they would treat any other grandparent or parent, though with a touch of deference.

When my sister and I reached the Circuit House the morning of that 19th November, we were told that Indiraji had gone to The Doon School to fetch her sons and would thereafter, take the boys to Kwality restaurant for a treat. We instantly decided that the restaurant would be a better option for our rendezvous with Indiraji. Putting our cycles in the reverse gear, we reached the restaurant in twenty minutes.

Diffidently, we approached Indiraji's table, unsure of the 'reception' since I felt we were trying to intrude in on family privacy. Indiraji looked up curiously; I nervously blurted out 'Happy birthday, Indiraji'. My sister took out the special blouse that she had knitted and I presented it to Indira Gandhi on her behalf. She graciously accepted the gift and asked my sister how did she know of her measurements. She mumbled something in response. Indiraji then asked us to be seated. We then joined India's first family as its 'gate-crashed' guests. Mrs Gandhi did not recall our name, she introduced me as a young journalist to her sons. I don't now remember how the two boys had responded but I found them preoccupied in eating ice-cream. A pound of stick-jaws, popularly known as Kwality toffees, had been ordered and delivered for the boys. From then onwards, I made sure that Indiraji remembered our names.

After his invitation, I must have subsequently met Pandit Nehru on five or six occasions in Dehra Dun. Once, I accompanied him on his visit to a village called Tuini in Chakrata. The front doors in the houses there were too low and The *Vanguard* then published a photograph of Pandit Nehru entering a house half-bent. When someone asked for the development of the backward Jaunsar Bawar area, Pandit Nehru delivered a long speech making out a strong case for what he then described as 'integrated development of the whole country' rather than piecemeal growth of individual areas. In an open letter in The *Vanguard*, I mustered enough courage and marshalled many arguments to challenge Pandit Nehru's premise of 'integrated development'.

Another, interesting encounter with Nehru, however, came about in Delhi. As a young reporter on the staff of the *Indian Express*, my regular 'beat' was Delhi University. The Students' Union of Irwin College (Sikandra Road) had invited Nehruji for some function. At the conclusion, scores of girls approached Panditji for his autograph. He graciously allowed only five minutes to autograph hunters, since, he claimed he had an important meeting to attend.

Long after the queue of autograph-seekers had vanished, Nehru was still there; he sat cross-legged on the dias, surrounded by a bevy of young, beautiful things chatting and joking. He had totally forgotten about his important appointment. In fact, I had never seen Nehru so relaxed, bantering and innocently flirting with the cream of Lady Irwin girls. I sat on the steps to the podium, watching Nehru at his flirtatious best. Then, he looked at me; there was a mischievous smile on his face, as if challenging a young man much less than half his age. All I could say loudly was, 'Sir, I really envy you'. And, thus ended this dream-like hour.

# Reading and Books in the Valley

Upendra Arora

It's in the air. There is something almost magical about this valley of ours, green and serene, with a delicate web of little rivulets and dry riverbeds strewn like necklaces across its terrain. Tucked in warmly between the great mountain ranges on one side and India's sacred river on the other, Dehra Dun, or the Doon Valley, has always been a source of enchantment for the traveller, many of whom succumbed to the charm and made the valley their home. The Doon Valley was written about centuries ago, when it was a thick orchard of *litchi* and mango trees, that was traversed by people going further up to the mountains, later when wars were fought, and then, when Guru Ram Rai first set foot here. The history, sociology, geography and anthropology of the valley was extensively documented in books in the nineteenth century by acclaimed British authors because by then, the British had made it their summer home on the way to a cooler Mussoorie. These books written by Williams and Walton are considered as classics today, as they remain comprehensive and authentic texts of reference.

G.R.C. Williams was the first Superintendent of Dehra Dun. His immensely readable account of his times, *Memoir of Dehra Doon* (1872) was perhaps, written when the fountain pen had not come into existence! H.G. Walton recorded his innings in the valley in his book, *Gazetteer of Dehra Dun* (1911). Mussoorie and Dehra Dun have always shared a cosy co-habitation—books about the Doon Valley carry exhaustive information about the 'Queen of the Hills', and likewise, books about Mussoorie tell about the Doon that was. *The Story of Mussoorie* (1910) by F. Bodycott offers an interesting account of the valley as the British perceived it—they would reach the valley by road and train and then get porters to take them and their belongings on foot up the hills to Mussoorie.

Picturesque landscapes naturally lend themselves to intellectual creativity. The Doon Valley has been a place of retreat for writers, who like to surround themselves within the echoes of their literary imagination. Among contemporary authors who have made an indelible mark on the literary map of writing in the English language in India and those from Dehra Dun, there is a proud list we can boast of, and rightfully so. Pandit Nehru's niece, Nayantara Sahgal is an old resident of Dehra Dun. Her books, *Plans for Departure* and *Rich Like Us* among others, received critical acclaim internationally when they were published and still enjoy a large readership. Students of literature at university level in Uttarakhand and elsewhere are encouraged to study her body of work. In fact, Pandit Nehru wrote a great deal while he was in jail here in Dehra Dun during the freedom struggle. Now, internationally known for his books,

I. Allan Sealy also calls the valley his home. He began writing on travel, and his latest novel *Red* has been published internationally. Leading contemporary poet, Arvind Krishna Mehrotra also shares a close association with Dehra Dun and spends time here at his mother's home. Another writer who became well known for her writings and whose books have recently been reprinted is Nergis Dalal.

Not just Indians, the valley has stolen the hearts of people from across the seas as well, who chose to make the valley their home and went on to pen their experiences. Two authors who come to mind instantly are Lewis King and David Keeling. Lewis led a most incredible life, having travelled the world the crazy way—and having done that, he still chose the valley to build his home and knit a family of the friends he made. His controversial book, *The Twentieth Century Heretic* questions a range of existing notions of time, space and existence. David Keeling, a former member of the British Foreign Service, retired to build an English style cottage in Dehra Dun. The *Asian Age,* carried a weekly column by him where he wrote joyously amusing anecdotes about the valley and its residents, with a typical whiff of witty British humour. His writings have been published as a collection titled *Doon on a Sunday.*

The valley has always been a seat of learning, as it is home to the finest educational institutions in the country. The Indian Military Academy trains young cadets, the Forest Research Institute is at the helm of research in ecological issues in India, the Wildlife Institute of India is internationally acclaimed for its efforts in protecting the flora and fauna of the subcontinent. One of the oldest institutions in the country, the Trignometrical Survey of India (TSI) has its headquarters here. Well-known and highly respected travel writer, Peter Hopkirk, came looking for information at TSI when he was working on his book, *Quest for Kim*. With a little help from this writer, he was able to go around the museum to pay his tributes to the great Indian cartographers and surveyors. His book praises his visit to the valley. He writes of his memorable experience at TSI and the help he received in making this possible. Henrich Harrer too, in his book, *Seven Years in Tibet* tells of his understanding of life in the valley where he interned during the Second World War.

Apart from the intensely special symbiotic and symbolic relationship the valley has shared with local, national and international authors, there is also a complimentary culture of reading. Our family-run bookstore in Dehra Dun has grown, matured and developed, just like the readers of our town and the town itself. Thirty-five years ago, ours was a little bookstore on the first floor of the two-floor building we are in today. Gradually, we began recording more orders, needed more space, so we moved downstairs, to a room quarter the size of the current bookstore. A few years down, we had an increasing clientele, more books being published, more books being read, more books being ordered. We needed more shelf space, so we bought the shop next to ours, which belonged to a photographer who ran his studio from there. So many books after and to this day, we still need more shelf space, for the wide array of subjects we are required to stock, for the various readers who visit our store. While many like the standard page-turners in the bestsellers lists each month, we have an equal number of readers, asking for travel and religion, self-help and muscle building, patriarchy and anarchy. It's all a good sign. As long as people like to read, my grandfather often said to us, there is hope for a better tomorrow.

Our bookstore is a small seed my grandfather planted in Dehra Dun, which my father and his brothers began to run in

INDIA
Life

the years shortly after Independence. The family tree of the bookstore traces back to Ferozpur Cantt in Punjab, where my grandfather ran a very large bookstore and trained us all. Today, my grandfather, Lala Narain Das is considered the founder of the book trade in India. Once he was confident of the training imparted, he sent each boy of the family out to a town in the country, to sow the seed of learning, to nurture it with the values he engrained, and to give back to the society around him.

For my father, just like it was for his father, a book is always like a friend. And, booklovers thus are all friends. Our bookstore has always been a meeting place for thinking minds, a watering hole for the intellectually thirsty. Over the years, sitting behind the counter at the bookstore, I have had the privilege of meeting most of Dehra Dun's reading (and hence, thinking) public, its new and growing population, its ambitious adolescents and its nostalgic elders. Through these daily interactions, I have felt the pulse of a valley slowly spread its wings and grow into a town, a town that has learnt to adjust to the needs of its citizens and found itself on the national map as a city that has groomed itself, to become the capital of the hill state of Uttarakhand.

The days that I was at college, helping my father run the store after my lectures, there was a film theatre adjacent to our bookstore. It was called the Odeon Cinema and in those days, it ran English films. That was something the residents looked forward to, and before the show, the regulars would drop in at the bookstore to chat, browse and buy their books. We would get the odd phone call from a customer, requesting us to buy tickets for him for the next show because he was running late, or sometimes much before time for the matinee because he didn't want to miss a chance to watch the screening. For a particular customer, we had standing orders to buy two tickets for the first day first show, irrespective of the screening! There were an equal number of people, who initially did not necessary enjoy reading, but because there was time before the film, they would have no option but to wander in and browse and who over time, began visiting the bookstore as a matter of routine, long after the Cinema was broken down and made into the hotel that it is today.

We still have people dropping in, every other day, asking what happened to the Cinema or reminiscing of those simple and enjoyable evenings. These are either people who moved out then to find greener pastures and returned in remembrance of things past or those that have now retired and settled around the valley and visit the bookstore to refresh the memories of their youth spent here. Books about the area that tell the tales of the times that were are very popular. India's well-known author and someone the writer and our bookstore are fortunate to have as a friend, and a well-wisher, Ruskin Bond, first lived in Dehra Dun. His books talk of the verdant valley and of Mussoorie as it once used to be. He has the rare gift of being able to weave stories that appeal to all ages—young children, teenagers, and adults—and thus, his writing has immortalised the valley and the hill station of Mussoorie in the imagination of readers, forever. He is a master storyteller and commands a readership from ages seven to seventy, which is quite rare for contemporary writing in the world today. The valley now shares a very deep association with him, and his books not only have a huge readership in Dehra Dun and among visitors to the valley, but also across the country and other parts of the world.

Khushwant Singh, in his famous column, once wrote most judiciously, that the bookshops of a town are the barometer with which we can justly measure the intellectual strength of a city.

And, after a book signing function at our bookstore, he carried a mention about it in the preceding week praising our collection of books. He thought, we were better stocked than most other cities he had been to. What better reflection of the valley's citizens than that!

The valley is famous for its educational institutions for the young—public schools like The Doon School and Welhams rank amongst the best and are deeply steeped in history. Their students have gone on to make a name for themselves in various spheres of life. Indira Gandhi used to visit Dehra Dun with her father. Her love for books brought her to our bookstore regularly. Later, she enrolled her sons at The Doon School and would visit our bookstore when she came down to see them. Even when she became Prime Minister and much after that, she chose to order her books from our bookstore. One of the main attributes of our old and cherished relationship with Indira Gandhi was her love for the environment. Since we publish and stock books on ecological issues, she was always keen to encourage and support us to help the larger cause of conservation. She passed her enthusiasm for reading and protection of the environment down to her son Rajiv, who carried on the legacy. He continued to patronise the bookstore much after.

Since teaching and education carry a great emphasis, the valley has always enjoyed an intellectual air. Schools use written literature as a source of study; children are encouraged to learn more through books. They are taught to develop the reading habit to widen their knowledge of the world. Since we have educational institutions, we naturally have educationists, and they too, are driven by a quest for learning. Literature, politics, art, defence and military affairs, ecology and environment, anthropology and history are all subjects that have readers.

Dehra Dun has always been home to citizens who perceive the world through the pages of the books they read. It is a place where most people dream of spending their old age, by a cosy fire in winter, huddled on a rocking chair, curled around a book. This is one reason the city has blossomed—retired educationists, environmentalists, government employees and army officials choose Dehra Dun over other cities to settle down in their old age. They bring with them the knowledge and wisdom that experience unfolds—making the city a 'thinking' one, one that is conscientious and mindful. They are aware of its rich natural, architectural and intellectual heritage and work towards preserving it.

Such social activism is not possible without a constant sense of awareness and understanding of the changing times. This is what books and literature provide—and we can proudly boast that in this supersonic age of cyber-rule, our quaint valley of grey hair and green hedges, we has three general bookstores and several others that stock other specialised subjects. Most evenings, these bookstores are buzzing with browsers, steaming with debate and discussion.

That is one of the myriad reasons for the increasing number of tourists to the valley. Since our bookstore is listed in the Lonely Planet Guide for India, we often find ourselves providing necessary tourist information about transport, accommodation and food to customers, and quite happily so! The nature of a good bookstore reflects the internal countenance of a city—just like Cambridge and Oxford are both centres of learning that can boast of their bookstores—Cambridge for Heffers' and Oxford for its Blackwells, we find solace in the pride our citizens display in our bookstore.

Dehra Dun has always been a sophisticated town of thinkers and thinking. It continues to be a town that cherishes a reputation, for its emphasis on education and learning. It is a shiningly optimistic sign for future generations, on this otherwise rather bumpy road of the not-so-distant future of altering forms of information.

# Saga of a Soldier

Ruskin Bond

When I look out of my study window in Landour, the first thing I notice is the 'Mullingar', a cluster of old, rather dilapidated buildings on a spur, overlooking the Doon Valley. Beyond it, in the hazy blue distance, I can see the small, forested hill of Kalinga, where the Gurkhas held out so valiantly against a British force commanded by Sir Rollo Gillespie, a veteran, who had fought several successful campaigns in South India, Java and the West Indies.

The Anglo–Nepalese war (1812–1815) was lingering on and it was imperative that the British take control of the Doon, Garhwal and Kumaon, which had been under Gurkha occupation for over a decade. The last British outpost was at Saharanpur, and it was from here that a considerable force set out for Dehra Dun, advancing through the Timli Pass. However, the Gurkha garrison at Kalinga repulsed several British attacks, and in one of them, Sir Rollo was struck through the heart by a musket ball. He died in the arms of his young A.D.C., Lieutenant Young.

And, as far as Lieutenant Young is concerned, that was only the beginning of a fascinating story—for not only did he go on to raise the first Gurkha regiment (made up of the brave survivors of the Nepali forces), he was also the founder of the twin hill-stations of Landour and Mussoorie, and the first man to introduce potatoes in the Himalayas!

Frederick Young was born in 1786 at Green Castle, Moville, in the north of Ireland. His forebears were English settlers, who had come over from Devonshire in the 17th century and his father and grandparents were clergymen. But Young wanted a life of travel and adventure, and so, at the age of fifteen, he joined the 2nd N.I. as a cadet.

The entrance examination/interview was brief and to the point:

'How old are you?' asked a member of the board.

'Fifteen, on 30th November last.'

'Are you ready to die for your King and Country?'

'I am.'

'That will do.'

He had passed. And so, under the aegis of the East India Company, he was to serve King and Country for forty-four years without a break.

Ensign Young arrived at Calcutta in 1802. As a boy officer, he served under Lord Lake throughout the Central India campaigns. In January 1805, he was present at the abortive siege of the fortress of Bharatpur. While ascending a scaling ladder, Young fell from a considerable height into the ditch below, where he was soon covered by all sorts of falling debris. He had been given up or lost, when he finally appeared among

his comrades, 'a miserable object covered with mud and blood, but quite uninjured' (I quote from his daughter's memoir).

Then, in Java, serving under Colonel Gillespie, he was injured when a powder magazine exploded. He recalled the incident in his matter-of-fact manner: 'I was blown up in Java with Rollo Gillespie and given up for lost, but I came back all right.' After the capture of Jakarta, the official report read: 'I regret to say that Gillespie himself was wounded in the left arm very severely, but not dangerously. Our loss, on the whole, has been considerable. Lt Young and Lt Hunter were blown up and much burnt, but not dangerously.'

We now come to the war with Nepal and General Gillespie's invasion of the Doon. The force under his command, advanced through the Timli Pass and made straight for the Kalinga entrenchment. But someone blundered, and the main force had to return, after a considerable loss in officers and men. Gillespie then led an assault with his old regiment, the Royal Irish Dragoons, assisted by two six-pounders. The desperate and brave Gurkha defence repulsed this and successive assaults, and Gillespie was killed in the fighting. Kalinga was never captured. It was entered only after it had been evacuated, and then, it was razed to the ground.

Lt Young, with a large body of irregular troops, then marched to Jaitak, near Nahan, to intercept the Gurkhas there. The force was routed, and Lt Young and a few of his officers found themselves deserted and alone among the enemy.

General Young's daughter, L. Hadow Jenkins tells the story: 'With taunts and jeers, the little hill-men surrounded them and pointed to the fleeing crowd: "What?" they said, "you here? See your soldiers are running away! Why not run after them?"...Young looked steadily at them with his fearless Irish eyes and said: "I did not come so far to run away. I came to stop." And, he sat down on the rocky hillside.'

He was now their prisoner, but they treated him with every mark of honour, as a brave foe. During the time he spent with them, he 'became intimately conversant with their language, he studied their religion, their prejudices, their manners and customs, and gained their friendship and admiration'.

When the war was over and the remnants of the Gurkha army had finally surrendered, Young immediately went about enlisting these disbanded soldiers, in what was to be known as the Gurkha Brigade or Sirmur Rifles. Given the authority from an appreciative government, he went to the prison camps at Saharanpur, told the men they were free and asked them to volunteer for service with the Company. His own proud words were: 'I went there one man and came out 3,000.'

So began the saga of the Gurkha soldier—in the Company's forces, in the army of the British Raj, in the Indian and British armies—regiments that were to distinguish themselves over the years, in campaigns in India and abroad, and in Europe during the two World Wars. To Young goes the credit for seeing their potential as fighting men, and for organising the Gurkha Brigades with their headquarters in Dehra Dun.

His organising abilities were appreciated to the extent that now a Colonel, he was appointed Superintendent of the Doon, with both civil and military authority, in the expanding town of Dehra Dun, the tribal tracts of Jaunsar along the Jamuna, and the embryo hill-stations of Mussoorie and Landour.

Young can be said to be the founder of Landour, when he set up a Convalescent Depot for ailing British soldiers in 1826. On a spur of the mountain, he built his cottage of 'Mullingar', where he spent part of the year and cultivated his famous potato garden.

Young was the first man to introduce the humble potato in the Himlayan foothills. This staple of Irish diet, he felt, would adapt well to Indian conditions. And, how right he was! His model potato garden was soon being duplicated in villages throughout Kumaon, Garhwal and the hill-stations, as far as the Sutlej. It's hard to imagine that this humble root vegetable, so essential a part of many an Indian dish today, played no role in the Indian cuisine, two hundred years ago.

Young's daughter spent her first five years in Mussoorie and Dehra Dun, and in her memoirs she recalls the potato garden, the ride up to Mussoorie from Rajpur, the parades on Dehra's huge parade ground, and the house her father built in a meadow off Rajpur Road where the St Joseph's Academy stands today.

Anyone seeing Dehra's parade ground today, would have a hard time, visualising it as it was in earlier times. The cantonment was, of course, shifted to its present site in the 1860s, but even when I was a boy in the 1940s, I remember the parade ground as being one vast *maidan* without any of the clutter, potholes, impediments and invasive structures that have turned it into just another waste ground.

In 1825, Young married the beautiful Jeanette: 'Colonel Frederick Young, Colonel of the Sirmoor Battalion of Gurkha Rifles, married Jeannette, the daughter of Colonel and Mrs Bird.' So went the official announcement. She was a splendid rider and shared her husband's love for animals. Her favourite chestnut Arab is seen in the foreground of the picture of their home in Dehra.

They had four children during the years. Young was Superintendent of the Doon. They were both sad to leave the Doon, then a beautiful unspoilt valley, where they had spent many happy and productive years, popular with all sections of society.

Young's tenure in Dehra ended in 1844 and, after serving briefly in Darjeeling and Dimapore, he came home to Ireland as a General.

His wife, Jeanette left a picture of General Young taking his last salute in Dimapore: 'Your papa looks very fine on parade. His charger is a handsome white Arab, and with the rich saddle cloth, and gold lace and all the corners embroidered in gold, it is a very gay affair! I attend all the reviews and inspections of troops with him and his staff. It is most amusing to see his five officers, all in cocked hats—dashing about after him! My horse always fidgets as if he thought he should be leading, too! The last morning I was out, all the Regiment drew up to play *God Save the Queen,* all together. I could not help laughing. The discord was great—one little fife playing louder than the others and one big drum quite silent. Indeed, it made all the officers smile; there is another monster review tomorrow and, of course, I am going to it.'

Young spent his last years in Ireland, where he died at the age of 87. He did not have an easy time in retirement, because in 1866, the Agra Bank collapsed and he lost all his savings and investments, but he still had his pension from the East India Company, so he was far from being a destitute.

There are no memorials to Young in Dehra or Mussoorie, but in the Dehra cantonment, there's still a Young Road, named after the regiment's first commander. There is also a Shakespeare Road, named not after the poet, but after one of Young's successors, Colonel Shakespeare, who took an interest in the local temple and was popularly known as Devi Sahib. His small son grew up in the Gurkha lines and was known as '*Devi Sahib ka Chhokra.*' But that's another story...

# Know More about Our Contributors

## David Keeling (1944–2007)

A writer, columnist and retired British diplomat, **David Keeling** was born on 5 July 1944 into a family of civil servants and farmers in Cheshire, England. It was his father's dream that he join the Foreign Service, which he eventually did. He first came to India in 1971 as a third secretary in the British High Commission in New Delhi. He met, and married Gauri Charatram, a daughter of the DCM family, in 1974.

David Keeling left New Delhi thereafter to work in various countries. He returned to India as first secretary in the 1980s. He became the head of press and information at the British High Commission in New Delhi. David took early retirement and settled down in Dehra Dun, where he built a home on Rajpur Road.

David Keeling was famous for his 'wonderful, dry, British, sense of humour' and his writings were characterised by this person whom he referred to by various names—Woman Friday and secretary in assistance.

He was planning a trip to Ireland before he breathed his last in 2007. He was sixty-two, and is survived by his wife Gauri and son Justin.

He has authored books like *Doon on a Sunday* and *Notes from Dehra Dun* and had been a regular columnist for *Asian Age*.

## Rakesh Bahadur

**Rakesh Bahadur** joined the IAS in 1979 after graduating *summa cum laude* and was allotted his home cadre, the then undivided U.P. He has worked in various capacities for the Government, in Uttaranchal, UP and the Centre. His preference, however, remains for the Himalayan hills, where he intends to settle down in his house at Ranikhet. He was District Magistrate of Dehra Dun during the early nineties, where this story is based. Till recently, he was Chairman of Noida and Greater Noida. When not working, he can usually be spotted playing golf or photographing birds.

## Arijit Banerji

**Arijit Banerji** was born in Kolkata and educated in Delhi, Dehra Dun and Kolkata. He spent his working life in the corporate sector. He worked in ICI, and was posted at various places in India and England. After retiring from ICI, he joined Haldia Petrochemicals Limited, from where he retired as Executive Vice President.

He has settled in Dehra Dun, and is involved with a school, a company, and an NGO. He spends a lot of time, solving puzzles and crosswords. His latest passion is reading up on Pakistan and claims to be well-versed with that country. His wife and two daughters, even though the latter have grown up and stay elsewhere, look after him. This is a full time hazardous occupation.

## Bikram Grewal

**Bikram Grewal** did his schooling at the famous Lawrence School, Sanawar, based in high the mountains of Himachal Pradesh before joining Delhi University, from where he has an MA in Modern Chinese History and Chinese Language. He has also been educated in England and America. Soon thereafter, he joined the prestigious publishing house of Longmans and was trained in their UK offices. Within a year, he was promoted to Regional Manager based at Delhi and later, as General Sales Manager. He then moved to British India Publications as Managing Director, before becoming the Indian representative of Dorling Kindersley. In 1995, he was asked to set up a full-fledged publishing and distribution company for them. In a few years, this became the largest publishing operations in Asia, employing over five hundred personnel, with eighteen offices in all major state capitals. In between, he has also worked in publishing companies Singapore and Hong Kong.

## Nayantara Sahgal

**Nayantara Sahgal** is the author of nine novels and eight works that affirm the values of cultural pluralism, religious tolerance and non-violence. Her novel, *Rich Like Us* was awarded the 'Sahitya Akademi Award and the Sinclair Prize. *Plans For Departure* won the Commonwealth Writers' Prize. She has served as Vice-President of the People's Union for Civil Liberties and as a delegate to the U.N. General Assembly. She has twice been Writer-in-Residence at Southern Methodist University, and held Fellowships at the Radcliffe Institute, the Woodrow Wilson International Centre for scholars, and the National Humanities Centre in the USA. In 1990, she was elected Member of the American Academy of Arts and Sciences, and in 1997, was awarded an Honorary Doctorate of Letters by the University of Leeds.

## Ramachandra Guha

**Ramachandra Guha** was born in Dehra Dun in 1958, and educated in Delhi and Kolkata. He has taught at the universities of Oslo, Stanford and Yale, and the Indian Institute of Science. He has been a Fellow of the Wissenschaftskolleg zu Berlin, and also served as the Indo-American Community Chair, Visiting Professor at the University of California at Berkeley.

Guha's books and essays have been translated into more than twenty languages. The prizes they have won include the UK Cricket Society's Literary Award and the Leopold-Hidy Prize of the American Society of Environmental History.

Presently, he has settled down in Bangalore as a full-time writer.

## Ganesh Saili

Professor **Ganesh Saili** was born in the foothills of the magical Himalayan ranges and has had the good fortune of living in the hill station of Mussoorie. From his perch, a mile high in the sky, for over thirty years he has written numerous books and contributed extensively on a range of subjects to prestigious journals in India and abroad. Ganesh teaches English and American literature at the local post-graduate college and is a professional photographer.

## Himmat S. Dhillon

**Himmat S. Dhillon** teaches English and Literature to senior classes at The Doon School, Dehra Dun. He also functions as Housemaster of Oberoi 'A' House. Earlier, he had passed out from The Lawrence School, Sanawar in 1989. He completed his graduation and post-graduation in English Literature from the University of Delhi.

He has worked as Editor with Harper Collins Publishers India. To his credit, he has a number of published articles, book reviews, travelogues and photo features in the *Times of India, Hindu, Economic Times, Statesman, Pioneer, Hindustan Times, Tribune* and *Asian Age,* as well as in *Down to Earth,* on a regular basis.

He has a varied interest as in Photography, painting, travel, reading, swimming, kayaking, trekking, bird watching, research on heritage sites and remote regions, coin and stamp collecting.

## Sumanta Banerjee

Born and educated in Kolkata, **Sumanta Banerjee,** was a journalist with the *Statesman* in Kolkata and New Delhi from 1962 to 1973. He is at present based in Dehra Dun, and is engaged in researching into the social history and popular culture of 19th-century Bengal. He is the author of several books, including *India's Simmering Revolution; The Parlour and the Streets: Elite and Popular Culture in Nineteenth-century Calcutta;*

*Under the Raj: Prostitution in Colonial Bengal*; and *Crime and Urbanization: Calcutta in the Nineteenth Century.*

## Kunal Verma

**Kunal Verma** is one of the country's most experienced aerial photographers, having logged hundreds of flying hours with the Army, Navy and Air Force in particular. Educated at The Doon School and Madras Christian College, he had a hand in opening up some of the trans-Himalayan routes from the Kashmir Valley into Zanskar and Ladakh while working with Tiger Tops, before switching to journalism and filmmaking. In the mid-1980s, he shot the bulk of the *Project Tiger* serial and has subsequently travelled extensively throughout the subcontinent, shooting both on the ground and from the air.

Apart from producing several highly acclaimed films that include *Salt of the Earth* (History of the IAF), *The Standard Bearers* (National Defence Academy), *Making of a Warrior* (Indian Military Academy ), *The Kargil War*, and *Aakash Yodha,* he is also the author of *Ocean to Sky: India from the Air* and was the chief photographer for the *Indian Navy: A Photo-Essay*. He has also shot the films on the Light Combat Aircraft, the Saras and most recently, the film on the Army War College in Mhow. He lives in DLF, Gurgaon with his wife Dipti, and their two daughters.

## Florence Pandhi

**Florence Pandhi** was born in 1945. She did her B.Sc., from Manchester University; SRN, Royal College of Nurses; SCM, Royal College of Midwives; and ONC, Royal College of Nurses,

U.K. At present, she is involved in social and environmental issues. She is Member of the 'Supreme Court Monitoring Committee' which supervises reclamation of the limestone mines in the Doon Valley, and to oversee the restoration of natural normalcy to the Doon Valley. She was also the founder-member, present Secretary and erstwhile President of 'The Friends of The Doon Society', the first environment society formed in the Doon Valley, actively working towards preserving its environment through education and social activism. She is Editor of its bi-annual publication. She is the founder-member of the 'Citizens Action Group' dealing with urban issues. She is also the Trustee of the John Martyn Memorial Trust.

## Karan Thapar

**Karan Thapar,** born on 22 November 1955 in Srinagar, India, is one of India's noted television commentators and interviewers. Currently, the President of Infotainment Television, Thapar is noted for his aggressive interviews with leading politicians and celebrities. In December 2003, he became the first person to win both awards in the current affairs category of the Asian Television Awards. His interview with Pakistan's Foreign Minister, Khurshid Kasuri, on *Court Martial* won 'The Best Current Affairs Programme'. He received his second award for 'The Best Current Affairs Presenter' for his popular long-running BBC series *Face to Face.* In 2005, he won the 'Best Current Affairs Presenter' for the third time since 1999 for his interview with former Indian Law Minister and BJP General Secretary Arun Jaitley on *HARDtalk India.* His other popular shows include *Eyewitness* (Doordarshan), *Tonight at 10* (CNBC) now India tonight—, *In Focus with Karan* and *Line of Fire.*

Thapar is also a prolific newspaper columnist. For instance, his weekly column, 'Sunday Sentiments' in the *Hindustan Times* is widely read. A collection of his columns has been published by the same name, *Sunday Sentiments*.

An alumnus of The Doon School and Stowe School, he graduated with a degree in Economics and Political Philosophy from Pembroke College, Cambridge in 1977. In the same year, he was President of the Cambridge Union. He subsequently attained a doctorate in International Relations from St Anthony's College, Oxford.

## Dev Lahiri

**Dev Lahiri** is an alumnus of St Stephen's, Delhi and Oxford University, and has been a Rhodes Scholar. He has headed several front-rank schools countrywide with distinction, leaving his special stamp and impress upon them.

Lahiri's major contribution to Indian education is the introduction of best corporate administration practices into school management. After returning from Oxford where he read social sciences between 1975–78, Lahiri worked as an editor–manager with Oxford University Press for five years, Hindustan Lever for six months, before switching streams to join The Doon School as a junior teacher. In 1991, he was invited to head the highly rated Lawrence School, Lovedale (estb.1858), near Ooty in Tamil Nadu.

After a nine-year stint at Lawrence, Lovedale, he set up the Selaqui School in Dehra Dun. Two years later, he was called to Kolkata to put the city of joy's Heritage School on the rails before returning to Dehra Dun as principal of Welham Boys School (estb. 1937).

## Irwin Allan Sealy

One of India's post-Independence writers, I Allan Sealy was born in 1951 Allahabad, Uttar Pradesh. After schooling in Lucknow, he attended Delhi University, then studied and worked in the United States, Australia, Canada, and New Zealand. Now, he spends much of his time in Dehra Dun. His eye for places, and his evocative descriptions are apparent in all his novels and in his travelogue, *From Yukon to Yukatan.* Sealy's first novel, *The Trotter-Nama: A Chronicle*, is a tale of seven generations of an Anglo-Indian family. *The Everest Hotel: A Calendar*, gained him an international following after being short-listed for the Booker Prize in 1998. His other novels are *Hero: A fable, The Brainfever Bird,* and his most recent novel is called *Red.*

Allan Sealy has won a number of awards for his writing, including the Commonwealth Best Book Award in 1989, Sahitya Akademi Award in 1991 and the Crossword Book Award in 1998.

## Victor Banerjee

Victor Banerjee was born on 15 October 1946, and is a British educated, Kolkata-based Indian film actor. He was born in a distinguished Bengali family. He is the descendant of W.C. Banerjee, a leading intellectual, a prominent man of his time and the first president of the Indian National Congress (1885). He had his schooling in St Edmunds', Shillong and graduated in English Literature from St Xaviers' College, Kolkata.

His most visible role has been in David Lean's *A Passage to India* (1984). He has also acted in Merchant Ivory Productions'

*Hullabaloo Over Georgie and Bonnie's Pictures* and Satyajit Ray's *Ghare Baire*. Though in recent years, he has largely been involved with Bollywood, he is also affiliated with the Bengali film industry. He also plays 'character actor' roles from time to time in the British cinema. He was also cast in the role of Jesus by director Stephen Pimlott in the 1988 production of the York Mystery Plays.

When not in Kolkata, he is to be found in the hill station of Landour in the Lower Western Himalayas in northern India.

## Bill Aitken

**William McKay (Bill) Aitken** was born in Scotland in 1934, studied comparative religion at Leeds University and hitch-hiked overland to India in 1959. He worked as a teacher in Kolkata, a gardener in a Gandhian ashram in Kausani and as *pakshastri* in a nearby Vaishnav temple. After twelve years spent in the Kumaun hills, he became a naturalised Indian citizen and moved to Garhwal as secretary to a maharani. As a travel writer, he has been to all the four corners of India by the erstwhile metre-gauge railway. He is an honorary member of the Himalayan Club and president of Friends of the National Rail Museum. His books include: *Seven Sacred Rivers, Nanda Devi Affair, Riding the Ranges, Footloose in the Himalaya, Touching Upon the Himalaya, Mountain Delight, Zanskar, 1000 Himalayan Quiz, Exploring Indian Railways, Branch Line to Eternity, Literary Trails, Divining the Deccan, Sri Sathya Sai Baba.*

## Palash Krishna Mehrotra

**Palash Krishna Mehrotra** was born in Bombay in 1975 and educated at St Stephen's College, Delhi, the Delhi School of

Economics and Balliol College, Oxford. He is represented in *First Proof : The Penguin Book of New Writing from India*, and is currently writing a book on contemporary India to be published by Rupa and Portobello Books, London. He lives in Dehra Dun with his grandmother.

## Raj Kanwar

**Raj Kanwar** has been a journalist, public relations/advertising professional and a businessman at different stages in his eventful career-span of fifty-five years.

He voluntarily retired in 2000 as the chairman of SK Oilfield Equipment Co. Pvt. Ltd., a family-owned business, to return to his first love of reading and writing. His columns in *Garhwal Post* and the *Himachal Times* were hugely popular. He has also done freelance writing for some national English dailies.

In September 2004, Oil & Natural Gas Corporation Ltd. had commissioned Kanwar to write its history of fifty years. The book published by ONGC under the title *Upstream India* was formally released by Petroleum minister, Murli Deora on 14 August 2006 at a special golden jubilee function at Dehra Dun.

Kanwar, and Amber, his wife of forty-two years, live in Dehra Dun. Of their three children, two live in the USA, and the third, a son, is based at Mumbai, running the family business.

## Upendra Arora

**Upendra Arora** has found himself surrounded by books for as long as he can remember. Having had the good fortune of being born into a family that founded the book trade in India, he has been able to successfully breathe new life into his father's business and create a niche market for the books he specialises in. His family-run bookstore is today, a mecca for book-lovers across the world. One of India's most popular writers, Ruskin Bond has dedicated a book to him saying, he is one of the few people in the book trade who truly cares about the books he sells.

The Doon Valley has been home for Upendra, since the days he would run across the road from home to the school nearby. There were times that he remembers jumping the walls of the neighbours' houses to get to his maths lessons in the nearby locality. His parent's home was then surrounded by orchards. Today, the road between his house and the school he went to, is the main road connecting the city, blocked by traffic at all hours, the lanes behind his house have huge bungalows, and the area around his house is today, the biggest shopping mall in the state. His bookstore, however, remains just as it was when his father sat behind the counter. Some things thankfully never change.

In 2005, Upendra was awarded the Venu Menon National Award for Animal Welfare.

## Ruskin Bond

**Ruskin Bond,** well-known as one of India's best-loved and most prolific writers, has been writing novels, poetry, essays and short stories for over half a century. Apart from this, over the years, he has expertly compiled and edited a number of anthologies. For his outstanding literary contribution's he was awarded the John Llewellyn Rhys Memorial Prize in 1957, the Sahitya Akademi award in 1992 (for English writing in India) and the *Padma Shri* in 1999. His story *The Blue Umbrella* (Rupa) was recently filmed by Vishal Bhardwaj.

## *My Notes on the Green Valley*

## *My Notes on the Green Valley*

## *My Notes on the Green Valley*

# My Notes on the Green Valley

# My Notes on the Green Valley

## My Notes on the Green Valley